For Now And Always

By

Elizabeth Castle

Name: Castle, Elizabeth, author

Title: For Now And Always

Description: Series: The Heart's Way

Publisher: In The Air Publishing

Identifiers: ISBN 9781967731121 (ebook) | ISBN 9781967731138 (paperback) | ISBN 9798305567373 (amazon hardcover)

Cover Design by thebookcoverdesigner.com. Designer: betibup33

Chapter One

"That must be them." Hushed voices were all wondering the same thing; the whispers sounded loud in the quiet of the office.

Isabelle Masterson kept her head down, but her eyes were following the progression of her boss and the two men who had captured the office's attention. But it was only one of the two men she was watching. Through the lenses of her dark-rimmed glasses, her eyes watched his every movement. He still had the grace of a large cat, his long stride covering the distance of the lobby with a smooth stride and economy of movement. When he was a teenager, people took his disinterest in the goings-on around him as laziness. But she knew he was far from lazy.

Ever since her boss at The Gables had told her he had hired The Heart's Way Foundation, and that John Bannon was going to consult on this project, she had been full of nervous excitement. She'd been following the organization through local newspapers and national headlines, hoping to see a glimpse of John ever since. Some people said he was dangerous. Some people said he was a crook. Other people said he was generous. Yet others said he was a godsend. Depending on who you were, he could be all four of those things. John Bannon had little use for greedy people, people who used others to further their agendas and their wealth. Ironically it was his dislike of the wealthy who squandered what they had that had made him go to work for a very wealthy man. Emmett Trevor was a self-made millionaire who lost his wife to cancer. He had founded The Heart's Way Foundation as a tribute to his wife, who was a well-known philanthropist. John Bannon had been working for Emmett over the last five years, and he had a reputation for being tough to work for and rough around the edges. But Emmett was fond of saying to reporters that he kept John around because of those very traits. John was hard to please, and the results were better off for it.

Isabelle watched as he continued to cross the room, unable to keep her eyes off him. He was tall, though shorter than her boss. John topped off at six feet. Isabelle was six inches shorter than he was. She remembered the one time she'd stood close to him, and she'd had to lift her head to gaze up at him. She had been tall at thirteen, but he'd made her feel small and dainty.

His hair was still a shade somewhere between blond and brown. His hair looked brown, but when the light hit it, the blond shone through. He wore it cropped short these days. When he'd been younger, it had brushed his shoulders. She liked the short hair cropped to his skull. It made him look older, more mature. The dress slacks were also a new addition. He wore the dark gray trousers low on his waist, his crisp white shirt unbuttoned at the throat, the cuffs folded up but tucked in neatly. They were a far cry from the jeans and black t-shirt he had worn at eighteen.

His face was still not what most women would

consider handsome. His features were chiseled, his jaw square. There was no softness in his face, and none of his features could be considered at all feminine. Even the longer hair of his youth hadn't softened his looks. His eyes were hazel, a light brown with flecks of green. The grown Isabelle had been attracted to that face. He looked dependable, reliable, and, quite frankly, incredibly attractive in her eyes.

If she hadn't gotten a job with Gable, John Bannon would have remained a fond childhood memory. He had been a brief bright spot in what had been a difficult time. But like most childhood memories, she hadn't thought of John in years. Then six months ago she'd opened the newspaper Gable had given her, and there he was. John Bannon had matured, but there was no mistaking him. She had read the article half a dozen times, and with each reading, more and more memories of John had surfaced.

She hadn't had a crush on him, though the grown Isabelle couldn't say the same. She'd only been thirteen at the time, not quite ready for boys and budding romances. He'd been more like the big brother she wished she had. Her brother, Marcus, still haunted her nightmares, and John was his antithesis, then and now. Looking at him strolling through the office, heading toward her desk, she felt anything but sisterly toward him.

Gable had given her the article because he had decided The Heart's Way Foundation was going to be his project's saving grace. He'd asked her to research the organization so he could figure out the best way to approach them. Isabelle had researched the organization, and if her research on John gave her a little extra thrill, she was the only one who knew.

Isabelle's stomach clenched again as he came ever closer. He was still fit. He looked lean in his clothing, but she knew they masked broad shoulders and a sculpted chest. John had always been a physical person. He'd worked construction at sixteen with his father. Then he'd gone into the military. In the five years since he'd left, he hadn't gone soft.

Isabelle squared her shoulders and rose from her seat when the trio reached her desk. Gable Lockwood was a large man, one who intimidated others easily. Though Gable stood about four inches above both Emmett and John, Gable's presence didn't in any way diminish John's. John's stance and posture told anyone who was paying attention that he couldn't be bullied or intimidated. How well she remembered.

Gable gestured to Isabelle. "I'd like you to meet Isabelle Masterson. Ms. Masterson is my project coordinator. Nothing would get done around here without her."

Isabelle held out her hand, first to Emmett. He shook her hand enthusiastically. When she held her hand out to John, she watched him closely for a reaction. All he did was take her hand in a firm handshake. There was no sign of recognition in his eyes. Deep down she hadn't expected him to recognize her. She had been a young, gangly teenager the last time they had seen each other. Any resemblance to her younger self was superficial at best. Her eyes still might be an odd shade of lavender, and her hair might still be a honeyed blonde, but she was no longer pudgy; her hair was tamed with a pair of scissors and a flat iron, and she didn't have braces or acne.

"It's a real pleasure to meet both of you. I've been following your organization's work." Isabelle dropped her hand to her waist when John released her. She held it to her stomach, feeling embarrassingly giddy in his presence.

Emmett was the one who spoke. "It's very nice to meet you, Ms. Masterson. Mr. Lockwood has been telling me you're heading this project. If his praises are to be believed, then I look forward to working with you and your team."

"She'll live up to them and then some." Gable gestured to the room across the hall and addressed Isabelle. "Do you have a moment?"

"Certainly." Isabelle smoothed her plum-colored skirt and grabbed her laptop. "I've got the presentation ready."

Gable guided Emmett and John to the conference room, closing the door behind them. "I've been excited about this project. The medical center we have in mind is the biggest of its kind in the state. Isabelle has researched all the other centers similar to what I want, and I've been working on the perfect location. We finally have the funds we need to get started on the project. Donations have been harder and harder to obtain with the recession, but my events committee outdid themselves with our last fundraiser. The mayor has been a big proponent of the project, which helps. Mayor Dobson's ratings are high, and he has been vocal in the press and with the voters."

Isabelle turned on the coffee pot, listening to Gable. He and the mayor were friends and had been since childhood. She had met the mayor a time or two, and she had been impressed with him. She didn't pay much attention to politics, but in the last election, she had voted for him and would again.

"Mayor Dobson is also smoothing the way for the building permits. He has also agreed to head up the board of directors. We've got several other people lined up for the board." Isabelle handed Gable a cup of black coffee. "Can I get either of you a cup?"

Emmett shook his head. "I gave up caffeine. My daughter tells me I don't need it with my high blood pressure. I promised her I'd quit."

Isabelle turned to John.

"Black, please." John turned his attention back to Gable.

Isabelle nodded, the knot in her stomach growing. She remembered that voice. John had a deep voice. Now she found his baritone sexy. She poured him a cup and one for herself. She doctored hers before handing John his and taking a seat.

Gable began his part of the presentation. "The children's medical center we are proposing is quite ambitious. There can never be enough researchers, doctors, nurses, and therapists for these children. When I was trying to get help for my daughter, I was extremely frustrated. There were waitlists for the major medical facilities, problems with insurance when you finally did get an appointment, and the traveling was harder on my daughter than some of the treatments were. I'm hoping this facility can help alleviate some of the burden on the other facilities."

John sipped his coffee, half-listening to Gable Lockwood. John knew the man's daughter had been in a house fire. She had been staying with her grandparents when the old wiring in the house sparked a blaze. The elderly couple didn't realize their home was on fire until the blaze had consumed a large portion of it. The couple hadn't been able to get to their granddaughter. Thankfully the fire department was able to rescue the child, but not before she had inhaled a large volume of smoke, and the fire had burned her legs and back.

Gable went from funding homeless shelters and community centers to taking on the task of building a large, charitable medical center for children in the heart of the Midwest. Though there were a few children's charitable hospitals, as Gable had said, there could never be enough. But Gable was way out of his league, which is why he had called in The Heart's Way Foundation. Emmett was enthusiastic about the project. John was a bit more reserved. John offered his services only when he felt the cause was worthy, and the people behind the project were willing and able to commit to and complete the project. Some people were overly ambitious and had no idea of the monumental tasks they were taking on. And because John got results when he approved a project, Emmett let him choose the projects he worked on. Emmett would take on every proposal that came through his doors if he could. John tried to be the voice of reason. And when that didn't work, John assigned someone else in the organization to the project and focused his attention elsewhere.

Emmett's foundation, The Heart's Way, had the resources and contacts to make a center like the one Gable was proposing take flight. The organization helped small not-for-profit businesses find the funding and the resources they needed to get their projects up and running. In the case of Gable, he had a vision, one he was not equipped to make into a reality. He didn't have the suppliers or contractor contacts he needed to build the medical center, much less furnish it, staff it, and keep it up and running. He would need accounting services, legal services, building services, and staffing services. The Heart's Way could supply those things or point Gable in the right direction. Gable and his story had touched Emmett. But Gable's vision and drive were what impressed John. It took a lot to pull on John's heartstrings. Part of the reason John had agreed to listen to the proposal for this project was that it was rare for an organization this small to come to him with such a big undertaking. Most of the projects The Heart's Way Foundation helped were not so ambitious. This would be the biggest project John had undertaken during his time working for Emmett, but he had no doubt his people were up to the task.

John looked over at Isabelle, who was waiting patiently for her boss to stop talking. Gable was a talker, something John had figured out about five minutes after meeting the man. Emmett was nodding and making appropriate noises as he listened. Most of what Gable was telling them were things he'd heard before. John's attention drifted to Isabelle.

He guessed she was of average height when she kicked off her heels. She had a very pretty face. Her eyes were hidden behind her glasses, so he wasn't quite sure of their color. They looked blue from where he sat. Her lips were unpainted but full. It was her mouth that kept grabbing his attention. She had a small smile playing on her face as if she were amused by her boss. John had an urge to kiss that smile off her face, to see that lush mouth of hers flushed pink from his.

John tore his gaze from the attractive Ms. Masterson before she noticed him staring at her. Her purple suit fit her well. The skirt was modest, coming below her knees. Her pale pink blouse was covered by a loose-fitting matching jacket that he guessed disguised a trim figure. Her jewelry was discreet, and her makeup was minimal. She looked like a nice, small-town girl from a nice, small Midwest town. Exactly the type of woman he stayed away from: small-town girls with small-town ambitions and small-town ideas. John's dates were sophisticated, career-minded, and not clingy. Isabelle had commitment written all over her. She was the type of girl from the town he grew up in. Small town and small-minded. He'd escaped his hometown, escaped marriage-minded small-town girls, and joined the military after he turned eighteen and finished high school. From there he'd ended up in Los Angeles, as far from a small town as he could get. He'd been stationed in California for a time, and when it came to making a permanent home, he'd chosen the outskirts of Los Angeles and a job in the city.

There wasn't a ring on her finger, so he guessed she wasn't married. John liked to assess anyone he worked with, and Isabelle seemed easy to typecast. And since they would likely be working together, he wanted to get a handle on her and the type of person she was. Gable called her competent, hardworking, and easy on the eyes. John agreed with the third assessment, but the first two he would hold in reserve until he had a chance to see for himself.

John decided it was time to interrupt Gable. "What about you, Ms. Masterson? I know why Gable is dedicated to this project. How about you?"

Isabelle was startled when he spoke, but quickly composed herself. John had only spoken a couple of words since his arrival. He had always been quiet, watching what was going on around him without much participation.

"I'm dedicated to all of our projects. This one is particularly special to Mr. Lockwood, but I can empathize with him. My mother was in a home and getting her adequate care was difficult. I can't imagine what it must be like to not be able to get good care for your child. My heart breaks for what Gable and his wife went through. Are still going through. And to not be able to get the right care because you can't afford it is an abomination. But as Gable said, money talks, and it's no different when it comes to healthcare. If you want top-of-the-line care, you have to pay top-of-the-line prices. It seems grossly unfair."

Only part of what Isabelle said rang true, but John couldn't quite put his finger on what was wrong with her short speech. "How many projects like this have you done?"

"Like this one? None." Isabelle nervously tugged at the hem of her skirt. "I've been here a year now, and the projects I've done have been smaller. I helped the local shelter get a contractor to rebuild the sleeping quarters at cost. I also helped a local school find a cheaper food distributor, one that could supply healthier food. I actively help our community shelter organize its fundraisers. I'm afraid building a medical facility is out of my skill set."

"It's out of all of our skill sets, which is why we need The Heart's Way." Gable was glaring at John.

John halted Gable's tirade. Emmett just smiled at him, not fazed by John's abruptness. John knew he had insulted Isabelle's abilities, but he wanted answers to his questions. "I need to know how much I can rely on Ms. Masterson. I realize she is your project coordinator, but the projects you've done up until now are nothing like the project you are attempting to undertake. Helping a school out and organizing a fundraiser is not the same thing as building a medical center."

Isabelle opened her laptop and plugged it into the oversized television. She pulled up her proposal. "Why don't you look over what I've come up with before you pass judgment?"

Isabelle spent the next hour going over her proposal. She and Gable had worked together to put a visual presentation together. She outlined the center, its potential locations, and the vendors she had lined up with donations of supplies, food, and volunteers.

"We'll need the appropriate construction team, electricians, plumbers, and HVAC installers. I have decorators in mind for this job." Isabelle pulled up the names and samples of work the decorators had done for other projects. Slide after slide, she put forth Gable's vision. She was a decent graphic artist, so she ended the presentation with a graphic representation of the completed building.

John leaned back in his chair while Emmett told her

how impressed he was. John didn't speak, but Isabelle had impressed him with her proposal. She knew exactly what Gable and the team he'd assembled could and couldn't do. Isabelle seemed to know everyone in this town and who was capable of what. He could take this proposal back to his team and have them focus on the key areas where she saw the most need for their assistance.

Gable's phone rang, interrupting Isabelle's concluding remarks. "I need to take this."

John and Emmett watched as Gable left the room. They turned inquiring eyes back to Isabelle.

"That was his wife. His daughter Brittany had a doctor's appointment today. She's growing so fast, and now she needs procedures done to help the scar tissue stretch over her growing body. Her burns were extensive."

Emmett nodded. "I've met her. She's a real trooper. John didn't mean to insult you earlier."

Isabelle smiled at Emmett's kind words but turned back to her presentation, unable to look at John. She knew she lacked the abilities she needed to impress him. "I understand. You don't know me, and Mr. Bannon is right. I've not done projects like this one and he has. You have people working for you who could build this center from the ground up without my help. But that's not what you do. You try to equip the people working on the projects to be able to do it themselves."

Isabelle took a breath and faced John. "That's what I want from you. I want you to equip me to be able to handle this project. Once you're gone, there will still be work to be done. I realize it's not just building the center. There will be constant fundraising and constant updates and maintenance to the structure. I don't think Gable completely realizes the lifetime commitment he's making. But if anyone I know is willing to dedicate himself to the center, it's Gable."

"What about you? Are you willing to dedicate the rest of your life to this project?" John couldn't help the challenge in his tone.

"No. I'm not willing to dedicate the rest of my life to this project. But I'm willing to dedicate all my time and talent to this project so long as I work for Gable."

It was an honest answer, one John appreciated. "How did you end up working here?"

Isabelle didn't want to answer his question. Not only would it sound like she was tugging on his heartstrings, but she was also embarrassed to answer him. Her family's fall from grace was humiliating. And while he might not remember her, she remembered him. She was too ashamed to admit to him how she had ended up here.

John leaned back in his seat, wondering at her hesitation. Normally he wasn't interested in the personal lives of those he helped. There was something familiar about her, though they'd never met. His unprecedented interest in her had him repeating the question. "Well?"

"I applied for the job like anyone else. I wanted to work somewhere where what I did mattered. What I do matters here." It was the truth, though certainly not all of it.

"Yes, what you do here matters." Emmett interrupted and gestured to the screen in front of him. "I remember when I first opened the doors of my organization. I had your enthusiasm and the same desire to do something with my life that would matter when I was no longer around. Just don't let your desire to help others take over your life. You have to have balance."

Curiosity made her speak. "I've read about your career. As I said, I'm a fan. But two years ago, you almost closed the doors of your foundation. The press said you had a nervous breakdown, but I don't believe that."

Emmett laughed. "I read those same reports. No, I didn't have a nervous breakdown. What I had was a project that fell apart because the people involved were more interested in pocketing donations than investing in the future of their town. Unfortunately, the press was on the side of the organization misappropriating funds. Let's just say I was getting disillusioned. I was working hard to try to help people, and so many of them weren't looking for help. They were looking for handouts. Which was ironic because these people were supposed to be trying to help rebuild their communities. Instead, they were pawning off the work and taking the credit. I guess I got burnt out. John here put things back into perspective for me. I've put him in charge of choosing the projects we take on."

Isabelle looked back at John. "So that's why you asked if I was willing to dedicate my life to this project." Isabelle closed her laptop and rose. "My life is a bit much to ask for, but you have my promise I'll work hard. You'll find everyone on the staff to be hard workers and dedicated to the work they do. Gable's project is overly ambitious and we're out of our league. We need your help."

John rose. "That's why I'm agreeing to help. I'm very

particular about the projects I get involved in. Gable's pitch was impressive. And your presentation was well thought out. With luck on our side and a lot of hard work, we'll get the medical center off the ground."

Isabelle nodded, trying to keep her composure. She knew her presentation would determine whether or not the foundation took the job. It seemed she was successful. Trying to keep a huge grin off her face, she led both men out to the hall. "In that case, let me introduce you to the rest of the team."

John followed Isabelle as she walked Emmett through the office. They met several people, all of whom claimed to be fans of the foundation. Instead of being cloying and desperate, John felt genuine enthusiasm from the small team. The organization consisted of a dozen paid employees and a fair number of unpaid volunteers. Isabelle knew everyone's names and job titles. Gable hadn't been exaggerating when he said Isabelle was his right-hand man. As he met the team, each one had a problem or question for Isabelle. She patiently answered everyone's questions, signed forms, all the while keeping an eye out for Gable's return.

"I have to say you've impressed me, young lady." Emmett shook her hand. "John here is hard to impress, but you managed to impress him too."

John lifted an eyebrow at Emmett's assumption, but Emmett knew him well enough. Had he thought the project was a joke or a waste of time, they would have walked out. A contract had not been signed yet. John refused to sign anything until he'd met with the potential client's team and team leaders. But Isabelle had impressed him just as Gable had. She seemed dedicated to her job, but time would tell.

Gable found the three of them after all the introductions had been made. "So, what did you all think?"

Emmett held a hand out to Gable. "We're in."

Gable didn't bother to hide his whoop of satisfaction. "You have no idea what this means to me. To all of us. We should celebrate."

In short order, Isabelle found herself seated beside John at a posh restaurant in the heart of downtown. She tried to keep the giddy feeling in her belly under control. She declined a glass of wine when offered. The last thing she needed was alcohol in her system. She was trying hard not to stare at John, trying to keep her thigh from touching his on the bench seat, and was trying not to drink in the scent of his aftershave. The faint scent that mixed with John's body chemistry was heady. If she didn't get herself under control, she'd end up giggling like a silly teenager with her first crush.

Fortunately, she wasn't required to contribute much to the conversation. Emmett and Gable talked enough for all four of them. John, too, was quiet, looking a bit impatient for dinner to be over. When the group finally broke up, Gable took Isabelle back to the office to get her car, while Emmett and John took a cab back to their hotel.

"So, what did you think?" Gable flipped the lights on in the small office. Everyone else had left for the evening. Ever the gentleman, Gable escorted Isabelle up so she could grab her purse and laptop before walking her to her car.

"I think we're quite lucky. I had the feeling that if my

presentation hadn't been up to Mr. Bannon's standards, we would have been commiserating over drinks instead of celebrating."

"I got that same vibe. Emmett said he trusts John's judgment and that he would make the final decision. I was worried The Heart's Way wasn't going to be able to handle the project, but Emmett seemed confident at dinner."

Isabelle locked the doors behind them and headed for her car. "I researched them thoroughly before you approached them. It's been a while, but they've done projects this size before. It was before Mr. Bannon's time, but what I know of him in the press tells me he's up to the task."

"I'm worried about his gruff manner. He was rude." Gable opened her car door after she hit the lock on her remote.

"Yes, he was. Don't worry about it. I've dealt with worse. Remember Mrs. Miller? If I can handle her, I can handle anyone."

Gable laughed, as she knew he would. Mrs. Miller didn't top five feet, but she was a force to be reckoned with. Things went her way, or they didn't happen. Somehow Isabelle had steered Mrs. Miller in the direction she wanted her to go, with the older woman being none the wiser. John wouldn't be as easily manipulated, but she knew he was a reasonable man.

"I hope you're right. This project means the world to me and Caitlyn. Brittany might not benefit, but hundreds, hopefully thousands, will."

Caitlyn was Gable's wife of fifteen years. Brittany was

now twelve years old; the scars that marred her body were now six years old. It had taken almost that long for Gable to put the project together. With John's help, Isabelle vowed to make the center a success. Not only for Brittany but for children just like her.

Chapter Two

The contracts were signed, and the plans were underway. John had yet to return, though he was due back today. Two weeks ago, he sent a couple of people from his team, and they'd been underfoot since. Isabelle felt out of her element, and Cindy and Melissa had completely taken over. Cindy was The Heart's Way's legal advisor. She was going through the contracts Isabelle's team had put together with local vendors. Melissa was John's immediate project coordinator, the same role Isabelle provided to Gable. Melissa was setting up meetings, gathering as much information as she could about local businesses that might be helpful, and working with existing contractors to work out timelines.

Isabelle was answering their unending questions. She was feeling more like a secretary than a project coordinator. She had even been relegated to ordering lunch and making sure the coffee pot was filled at all times. In two weeks, the duo had turned the office upside down. Thankfully there were other projects in the works, and Isabelle spent a good portion of her day focusing on those, not on how useless she was feeling on this project.

"How are you holding up?" Gable stopped at Isabelle's desk, resting a hip on the edge of it while watching the chaos going on around him.

She ignored his question, knowing he'd never notice she didn't answer. "I'm finishing up the Langford project. How are you holding up?"

"It seems so surreal. We've been talking about this for so long, and it's amazing to see it finally coming together." Gable watched John's team work. "John's plane should be arriving any minute. I'm going to meet him at the hotel in a couple of hours. He's got a few more contracts for me to sign and a few details he wants to go over. Want to come?"

Isabelle nodded her head. The giddy part of her wanted to run out the door right now and meet him at the airport. The sane part of her said she could wait a couple of hours. "I'm just about finished here. Then I've got a call with Mildred about renting out the hall next month. I should be ready to go with you by the time he's settled."

"Good. You should have been an event planner. You book more fundraisers than anyone else around here. Fortunately, you're great at it." Gable stood. "How's your mom doing?"

The off-topic question was another question she didn't want to answer, but when it came to family, Gable would notice if she didn't answer. "I guess she's fine. She's currently not answering my phone calls. Nothing new there."

Gable grunted at that. His eyes were serious when he bent over her desk to keep their conversation quiet. "How did the hearing go?"

Isabelle shuddered and wrapped her arms around her waist. "Parole was granted."

Gable's eyes narrowed. "Figures. Our court system is so messed up. How could they let that creep out?"

Isabelle just shrugged her shoulders. "His lawyer argued he has proven he's rehabilitated, whatever that means. The parole board agreed."

"What are you going to do?"

Isabelle looked around to make sure no one was nearby. She still regretted opening up to Gable about her brother. But it wasn't like she could keep it a secret, not when Marcus made collect calls every month to the office through the main office line. She guessed his lawyer told him where she worked. Never mind that she never accepted the charges. She hadn't spoken to him since before his arrest. He still called like clockwork. Thankfully Gable was understanding. Her brother's constant phone calls had gotten her fired from her last job. Her boss hadn't wanted the sister of a convict working for them.

"Honestly, I don't know what to do. He knows where I work. I imagine in this day and age, it wouldn't be hard for him to find out where I live."

"You could get a restraining order."

Isabelle scoffed at that. "They don't work. His girlfriend got a restraining order against him. He broke that order in less than a week. Of course, he ended up in jail, but something tells me it wouldn't deter him."

Gable patted her shoulder. "If he comes around, I'll take care of it. Let me know if he tries to contact you. I'll come fetch you in a couple of hours."

Isabelle watched him leave. Gable had been so nice to her, but she had no intention of burdening him with her problems. She wasn't sure what Gable would do if he were confronted by her brother. She certainly didn't want to see him hurt or mixed up in her troubles.

Her brother Marcus had finally wound up in jail after beating his girlfriend. His lawyer had pleaded down the charges. Marcus agreed to a reduced jail sentence and agreed to get treatment for his anger issues. Isabelle was grateful the day he was put behind bars. That was only three years ago. He had been given a five-year sentence. The paperwork would take a little time, but Marcus would be released before the month was out.

Isabelle feared what he would do. She had testified as a character witness for the prosecution. Their mother still blamed her for turning against him. She guessed the moment he was released, he'd seek out their mother, not her. But he was vengeful. Isabelle had planned to be long gone when he was released, but that had never happened. Now she had a job she loved and wasn't about to let Marcus chase her off.

Isabelle finished her paperwork and made her phone call. By the time Gable came to fetch her, she had once again banished her family problems to the back of her mind. John, though he didn't know it, was a bright spot in her life right now. They had formed a reluctant friendship fifteen years ago. Reluctant on his part. Isabelle had been obnoxious but tenacious. She wasn't sure why she had wanted to befriend him so badly, but her teenage heart had been hanging on her sleeve when it came to him. But he'd been nice to her even though he and her brother were enemies. He'd been nice to her even though he hated her father and all her father stood for. He'd treated her as her own person, one of the only people she'd ever met who had.

"Ready?" Gable interrupted her thoughts of the past.

Isabelle tucked her laptop in her work bag and grabbed her purse and coat. The ride to the hotel was relatively short. Gable had gotten prime office space in the heart of downtown, another favor from the mayor. They entered the lobby, and Gable led her to the elevator. She had booked the rooms, so she knew where John was staying. She had booked two rooms. One for Melissa and Cindy, and one for John. Most of the work could be coordinated through teleconferences, but Emmett had told her John was a hands-on type of employee. Knowing John, that hadn't surprised her one bit.

John greeted Gable and Isabelle when they knocked on his door. John was not surprised to see her. It seemed Gable didn't go anywhere without her. This time she wore a teal pantsuit. She seemed to favor a lot of color. The slacks outlined her slender legs, and this jacket accentuated her waist instead of hiding it. The outfit suited her.

Despite not being surprised she was here, it was a bit disconcerting for him to see her. Since he'd met her, he'd been thinking about her at odd times of the day and night. She wasn't his type, but something about her was holding his attention, whether he liked it or not. He still couldn't shake the feeling he knew her. He hadn't had a chance to do a thorough background check on her yet, as was his custom when embarking on a project this size, but he was sure he'd remember if he'd met her before. What annoyed him was that she had invaded his dreams a couple of times. He didn't let women affect him, but Isabelle seemed to have slipped past his guard.

In some ways, she reminded him of the girls he grew up with. John didn't spend much time thinking about where he grew up, not having returned to his hometown in the heart of Kansas since he'd left for the military fifteen years ago. His parents retired to Arizona the year he graduated, and there was nothing else tying him to the place. The town had been filled with people who had hoped to see him fail. He hadn't, but he didn't care enough to go back and show them he'd succeeded. His teachers had written him off as a bad seed, and he'd gotten into more than his share of trouble. But to be fair, the trouble hadn't been all his fault. He certainly hadn't sought it out. He'd been the target of bullies, but they hadn't intimidated him. He'd held his own until that fateful day when they'd beat him within an inch of his life and left him bloodied on the school's football field.

John shook off the memory. Something about Ms. Masterson triggered memories of a childhood he'd just as soon forget. Or perhaps it was simply because his hometown was only about seventy-five miles south of the hotel room he now stood in.

"Come on in and make yourselves comfortable." John gestured to the sitting area.

Isabelle was still reeling from the way he had been staring at her. Whatever he'd been thinking about, it hadn't been pleasant. It broke her heart a little to see that slight anger directed her way, especially since she hadn't done anything to earn it.

Oblivious to either of the pairs' turmoil, Gable piped

up. "So how was the flight? I heard storms were predicted throughout the Great Plains."

John silently sighed, wishing he didn't have to make small talk. He had never been chatty, but he'd learned to make idle conversation with clients. "The flight was a little bumpy, but otherwise fine. The storms were further north."

Once Gable seemed done with chitchat, John dove into the project. "I've been in contact with some contractors I prefer to work with. They'll head the projects, using local crews. Cindy has been working on the contracts. The most pressing one is with the real estate agent and the seller of the property you've chosen to go with. You'll need to look all of them over with your board and sign. We'll want to break ground soon. Thankfully the winter has been mild, and the ground is not as frozen as it could be."

Isabelle took the printout of the contract from John. This was not her area of expertise, but she could understand the gist of it. She would have her legal expert look it over, but she did not doubt Cindy had put together an ironclad contract that would benefit both parties. The board had made the final decision of which property to go with last week, so they were set there. Final negotiations and closing shouldn't take too long. The seller was interested in their project and was willing to cut them a deal.

Isabelle was more worried about the local crews. "I'll make sure the board gets copies right away. I do need your help with the local construction firms. The bids to fix up one of the city's homeless shelters were much higher than we had budgeted for. It had taken two months of negotiations to get the bid down to an affordable amount."

John wasn't overly concerned. "This is a huge contract and whoever wins the final bid will come out ahead in the end. Just the publicity alone is worth winning the contract. We'll start taking bids as soon as my contractors are signed on. One man in particular, Jeff O'Connell, will make sure the bids are reasonable and he'll research the bidders. Also, he'll be at the site supervising the work. With Jeff, we won't have to worry about corners being cut or work not being done properly. His inspectors will monitor the entire project."

Isabelle nodded, grateful she wouldn't have to deal with the construction firms. She hated to admit it, but some of those men intimidated her. They used their physicality to try to force her to their will. She hadn't bent to their will, but the confrontations always left her shaky.

Next on the agenda was the warehouse. She was particularly pleased with the coup she pulled off. "I have another contract for Cindy to look over. We've been using a warehouse down by the river to store supplies and donations. The owner has been letting us use the space for the past year at a deep discount with the agreement he'd give us an official two-year lease if we got the deal for the center signed. I've got the lease agreement ready. And I'd like to take you over to the warehouse so you can see what materials we've got."

John took the contract. The amount they were paying to rent the 120,000 square foot facility was practically nothing. "And he agreed to the same amount fixed over the next two years? How did you pull that off?"

Gable was practically beaming. "Isabelle met him at the

local shelter where he was volunteering. When I hired Isabelle, she immediately thought of Stan when I mentioned storage. Stan Oakley owns several commercial buildings in the city. When Isabelle approached him and told him what the space was for, he said I could rent his waterfront property. It had been vacant for over six months and isn't in a great neighborhood. We keep a security guard on duty and put in new cameras. We'll leave the improvements we've made when we vacate. He was pleased to help with the project. He also knew the project wasn't up and running all the way, so he didn't make us sign a lease. We've been renting month to month. Now that we've got you on board, we can sign a more permanent contract."

Isabelle was fidgeting with her slacks. John was starting to believe it was a sign of nerves. She'd been toying with the hem of her skirt during her presentation two weeks ago, tugging at it as if to cover herself. John pulled his focus back to Gable. "I'd say we owe Mr. Oakley a debt of gratitude. You'd pay triple this back home, if not more."

Isabelle smiled at John, then dropped her gaze. She was glad Gable hadn't explained how she had met Stan. Isabelle had been living at the shelter at the time. She'd offered to volunteer during her stay there to try to pay back what had been given to her. That was how she'd met Stan. He was past the age when most men retired, but Stan was so full of energy and drive that she didn't think he'd ever slow down. He was new to volunteering, as was Isabelle, and they'd formed a friendship of sorts over the three months she'd been going there. And when she approached Stan about her new boss renting out one of his warehouses, he thought he was doing her a favor by helping her out in her new job. She'd certainly impressed Gable when, during her first week on the job, she'd rented an entire warehouse dirt cheap. She had tried not to take all the credit, but Gable insisted that if he hadn't hired her, he'd be paying top dollar somewhere else.

The three of them finished going through the contracts and the immediate plans. John would be coming into the office over the next week or so to iron out the rest of the details. Isabelle was glad the work was finally getting underway, and she'd have John in the office.

John glanced over at Isabelle. He'd caught her looking at him a few times, and he couldn't help wondering what was on her mind. And since she'd caught him looking at her a few times, he was glad the pair were taking their leave. She was working with him now, and it would be extremely inappropriate if he made a pass. But the way she got flustered and dropped her gaze when their eyes met made him wish he'd met her outside of work. The more he was around her, the more attracted to her he was becoming. And if it was this bad after only their second meeting, he wasn't sure how long his self-control would last in the future. This was at least a two-year commitment on his part, and two years seemed a long time to keep his hands to himself. He couldn't remember the last time a woman appealed to him half as much. He could only hope she'd end up being whiny and annoying. Whiny women were guaranteed to turn him off.

John waved them off and gratefully closed the door behind them.

Gable and Isabelle were in the elevator before Gable spoke. "So, what was with the googly eyes?"

Isabelle looked up at Gable, her confusion plain. "My what eyes?"

"You know, googly eyes. You were looking at him like he was the most fascinating thing you'd ever seen. It was odd, that's all. I've never seen you stare at a man before."

"I wasn't staring." But Isabelle knew she had been. And John had caught her more than once.

"There's nothing wrong with it, or anything. He's an attractive guy and you're a single gal. I just have never seen you mooning over a man before."

Isabelle wasn't sure how to answer Gable. She didn't want to admit she'd been staring. Ever since she'd seen his picture six months ago, she had found herself thinking about him at odd times. Having him in front of her in the flesh, and seeing that he still had all the traits she had admired in him when she was a young girl, made her notice that she was female. It had been so long since she'd felt attractive, and John made her senses sit up and take notice.

Isabelle sighed and pushed the button for the lobby. "Was it that noticeable?"

Gable laughed and patted her on the shoulder. "Sorry, but yeah, it was. He'd have to be completely blind not to have noticed the way you were admiring him."

Isabelle muttered under her breath. "This is a terrible time for my hormones to kick into gear. We just started work on this project, and I have at least the next two years to work with him."

"It could be worse. He could be your boss." Gable

gestured for her to precede him out of the elevator when the door opened.

"I suppose there's that." Isabelle hitched her purse higher and led the way out of the hotel. She couldn't help but look up toward the window where she knew John's room was located. "I don't know what's wrong with me. I can't tell you the last time a man attracted my attention half as much as John."

"Isabelle." Gable halted her and waited for her to face him. "You've had a rough few years. First, there was the mess with your brother. Then your mom. You lost your job and your home. When I met you, you were living in a shelter; that is when you weren't living in your car. You've come a long way this past year. Maybe it's time you found yourself some male companionship. You'd make a lucky guy a great wife."

Isabelle wiped impatiently at her tears. "I've been a wife. He's half the reason I ended up in that shelter. I'm not so sure I'm anxious to do that again."

Gable snorted at that. "Your ex-husband is a weenie."

Isabelle found she could laugh. "Yeah, the worst part is that I knew it when I married him. But it seemed like a good idea at the time."

"Now you've got a great job. You have your own apartment. You've been standing on your own two feet for the past four years. Maybe it's time to find someone you can trust to lean on once in a while, while still standing on your own two feet."

Which brought her thoughts back to John. How easily she could picture leaning on him. He wouldn't bail on his family when times were tough like Nathan had. Her husband had left her high and dry when he'd presented her with divorce papers, saying he was fed up with her family and was tired of taking care of her. To be honest, she couldn't blame him. He married her when she was nineteen, right after her father died. He'd spent the next six years putting up with her brother and financially supporting her mother. She did, however, take issue with his statement that he took care of her. She took care of their home and had a full-time job. If anyone took care of anyone, she took care of him. Yes, she had been desperate when she married him, but she had pulled her own weight in their marriage.

In the end, Nathan said she just wasn't worth the trouble. More than any of the other things he'd said to her when he'd walked out, that had hurt the most. Even his admission that he was having an affair with one of the women at his office and was moving in with her hadn't hurt as badly as saying she wasn't worth the trouble. She'd already been suspicious before he'd admitted to the affair; she just had been too scared to bring it up because she knew he wouldn't stick by her side if she confronted him about it. Her brother's arrest had simply moved up their divorce. She'd known it was inevitable, but she'd been scared to be alone.

But Gable was right. The past four years had made a lot of changes in her. She had moved out of the home she and her husband had rented and signed the divorce papers. They had come to a quick agreement, and neither of them contested the divorce. What she hadn't expected was that he would empty their joint bank account the minute their divorce was final and leave her with nothing. She'd struggled to make ends meet, and she'd managed for two years. At least she had until her brother had gotten her fired from her job.

Unable to pay her rent, her landlord had locked her out of her apartment. He'd allowed her back inside to grab her belongings, but that was all. And when she'd gone in to get her stuff, everything but her clothes had been stolen. She couldn't prove it was her landlord, but she knew it had been him. The police had been no help. The officer had simply given her the address of a local shelter and left her standing beside her car outside the apartment building. Ironically, the shelter was where she had met Stan, and he had let her use his address to apply for new jobs. When Gable had hired her, she had broken down in his office, sobbing into the tissue he'd given her, blurting out what had happened.

All of that seemed so long ago.

Isabelle got a grip on herself. "Next time, kick me under the table if I get googly eyed. I'm trying to pull off sophisticated and poised. John strikes me as the type of man who appreciates sophisticated women."

Gable laughed. "You are those things too, even when you are mooning over a man."

Chapter Three

"We've gotten some of our suppliers to donate materials. We've got tons of drywall, boxes of screws, and stacks of lumber. I've been working on trying to get some window suppliers, but I figured your guys should probably be involved in that." Isabelle waved at the security guard, unlocked the warehouse door, and disabled the alarm.

John waited, admiring Isabelle's legs in a pair of black tights. She was wearing a pair of heels again. He hadn't seen her in anything else. They did wonderful things to her legs, even when they were covered up. He was looking at her back when she turned around and waved him in. He patiently followed, glancing around the warehouse. She hadn't been kidding. There wasn't enough material to build the entire structure, but this would help the budget. He saw reams of electrical wire, metal fastenings, and even what looked like desks and chairs stacked in the back.

"I still don't know how Gable got so many donations." Isabelle pulled the door closed behind them, unbuttoning her coat while John looked around. The spacious warehouse wasn't yet filled, but it was almost half full. She had hopes of getting it filled to the rafters.

"Charm. And he's not shy." John headed toward the back, wondering what else was hidden behind all the materials. There were cinder blocks stacked several rows deep, sheets of glass wrapped in plastic, and pallets of insulation. There were stacks of plywood, various types of floor and ceiling tiles, and more stacks of wood than he could count. He imagined they could frame a large two-story house with what was sitting in the warehouse.

Isabelle thought about that for a minute, then couldn't stifle a laugh. "Gable is charming. He gets people to open their hearts and their wallets to his causes. And no, I don't think anyone would describe Gable as shy."

John was quiet for a moment before he spoke. "I do owe you an apology."

Isabelle turned startled eyes his way. She'd never seen John apologetic. He'd said many mean things to her trying to drive her away from him that fateful week fifteen years ago, and even after he'd relented and let her stay, he hadn't apologized. She wasn't sure she wanted him to start now.

"Don't worry about it." She looked away. "As I said, you don't know me."

"I've had this unshakable feeling that I do." John headed toward the office space in the back. He wanted to see the invoices. The neatly stacked supplies were a pleasant surprise, but he wanted to see the paperwork of ownership.

Isabelle was grateful that his back was to her. She gaped at him, surprised by what he'd said. Not once in the last week they had been working together had he hinted at any familiarity. She hurried after him. She skidded a bit on some old oil on the floor, slamming into John.

John quickly turned and held Isabelle steady. He

realized this was the first time he'd touched her, besides the handshake when they met. Her arm was firm in his grip. This close to her, he could see through her glasses that her eyes weren't blue; they were an odd shade of violet. Some distant memory stirred but didn't quite form. Her faint perfume filled his nostrils, and he could see she was breathing heavily, not only from her near fall, but because she was close to him. Her eyes were dilated, and she stared helplessly up at him. He knew she was attracted to him. It was hard not to tell when he'd catch her staring at him like she was right now; then she'd avert her head, trying to hide her blush. She was blushing now, but this time her gaze held his. But as cute as she was with flushed cheeks, he knew it was best to let her go.

"You really shouldn't wear heels in here." He let her go once she was steady on her feet. He held the office door open for her and gestured her inside.

Feeling incredibly embarrassed and a bit unsteady, she preceded him and went straight to the filing cabinet. Her heart was racing, and her arm was tingling where he had grabbed it. She took a moment to compose herself while she collected the thick file folders.

"Here is the itemized list of everything in the warehouse. I did a walk-through and took an inventory. I still haven't finished filing the invoices yet. Gable's previous project coordinator hadn't taken an inventory of the donations. He had simply filed the packing slips, estimated the value of the donations, and tossed the papers in the filing cabinet."

John glanced over the folders she held. "I'd have fired

him."

Isabelle nodded. "Gable forcefully suggested he should look for a new job. He promoted me to project coordinator when he left. Gable gave me the task of organizing the warehouse, but I haven't had much of a chance to finish the paperwork. I've spent most of the last couple of months finishing up current projects and putting the proposal together for your foundation."

"I can see why Gable put you in charge. You've certainly proven useful. When I start a new project, I'm never sure how it's going to go."

"My goal is to get these all scanned and organized. We had supplies all over the city. Some of the donors held onto the materials for us. But now that we have all this space, regular deliveries have been made so we could take possession. I think we're waiting on just a couple more shipments, so this is almost everything. We've had team members in and out of here the last couple of months, trying to organize everything. Thankfully one of the team members' nephews knows how to use a forklift. We rented one and had him come in and stack everything."

"You know you're rambling, right?" John couldn't help teasing her. She'd been very chatty this past week, telling him just about every detail of everything she'd done on this project.

Isabelle took a deep breath. "You make me nervous."

John's brows shot up at her admission. "I know. I didn't think you'd admit it."

"I think we need to get back to work before I say or do something stupid."

"Like?"

Isabelle could see the challenge in his eyes. She knew she should back off. John was not a man to mess with. And he was not a man to play games with. Isabelle had never learned to play the games other women did with men. She'd had two serious relationships in her past. One had been with her high school sweetheart, whom she'd adored. He'd eventually broken up with her when he met someone else after he went away to college. Then she'd married Nathan, who'd asked her to marry him when she needed help taking care of her family. That had ended with her disillusioned, and she couldn't say she'd ever loved him. That was the limit of her experience with men, at least romantically. John was far out of her league, and she knew it.

She wasn't quite sure what made her cross over to him. In her heels, her eyes were at the level of his mouth. If she stood on tiptoe, her mouth could easily reach his. Knowing she was crazy and was probably making a huge mistake, she placed one hand lightly on his chest and stood on her toes to kiss him. She kept the contact light, her eyes open on his. When he didn't return her kiss, she dropped back down on her heels, disappointment and embarrassment lighting her cheeks.

"You know this is a bad idea, right?" John took her wrist to keep her from backing away from him. She was no longer looking him in the eye. "We have a job to do, and sex complicates things."

Now highly embarrassed, she pulled her wrist from his grasp. "I don't recall asking to have sex with you."

His face was serious when he spoke. "No, you didn't.

But it starts with a kiss. Then it progresses to several kisses. In short order, we end up in bed. Then it gets awkward. You get mad because I'm not romantic and don't live up to some preconceived idea you have of what a business-slash-romantic relationship should look like. I'd want to keep our relationship professional at the office, and you'd want the whole world to know about us. And when things go sour, it becomes impossible to work together."

Something about what he was saying spoke of experience. "How many women that you worked with did you sleep with?"

"Just one. And I swore never to do it again." John let her go and took a step back to take a seat on the nearby desk.

Isabelle felt humiliated, and quite frankly, defeated. He sounded so sure. And she hadn't thought beyond kissing him. She should have. She was not naive. She knew what men wanted from women. If her relationship with her husband taught her nothing else, it taught her that. Her husband hadn't loved her, but he had wanted her physically; at least he had when he'd asked her to marry him. After their first year of marriage, their physical relationship was mostly nonexistent. And to be honest, she hadn't minded his disinterest. Something had always been missing from their physical relationship. In the end, she realized it wasn't sex he was disinterested in, but sex with her. She hadn't been surprised when he'd hooked up with another woman. And when she looked back, she wasn't surprised he'd left her to be with another woman, either.

John, on the other hand, was the polar opposite of her

ex-husband. She had no doubt his appetites were strong, but he wasn't the type of man to cheat. And she doubted that if she ever found herself in his bed, she'd feel disinterested. The real problem here was that he was not attracted to her the way she was to him. And though she hadn't thought beyond kissing him, he wasn't the one who spent the time they were together covering up covetous glances and embarrassed blushes. She had it worse than a teenager with her first crush.

And worse, now he knew it.

She managed to finish the tour of the warehouse without embarrassing herself again. He'd left the office and headed back out to take a brief catalog of the rest of the warehouse after the kiss. She'd remained behind for a moment, folders hugged against her chest, taking deep breaths to calm her heart rate. She'd made a fool of herself, and there was nothing she could do to take it back. All she could do now was stay away from him, avoid any physical contact, and talk about nothing but business.

They had finished the tour and were heading back to the car when her cell phone chirped. She fished it out of her bag and clicked the message button. The message was short and to the point. The number was unknown, and it simply said, "See you soon." Isabelle stumbled a bit and glanced at John, whose back was to her. She looked around up and down the street, but she didn't see a familiar face. Not wanting John to see her flustered, she pulled the hood of her coat over her head and quickly followed him to the vehicle.

Since she heard the ruling that her brother was to be released, she'd been dreading something like this. Her first fear was that he would show up at her job. Her second fear was that he'd show up at her apartment. And since there was no threat in the message, and she had no proof it was Marcus, she couldn't go to the police. As fear twisted in her belly, her first thought was to run. She could quickly pack up her things, toss them in her car, and drive far away. She had a small stash of cash. Being homeless had taught her to save her pennies. She could take that and just go.

Then Isabelle glanced over at John, who was expertly guiding the vehicle through city traffic, taking them back to the office. If she ran, she would never see him again. Though she supposed that might not be a bad idea either, after having kissed him and having been rejected. Her fear was warring with her embarrassment.

Isabelle managed to calm down by the time they reached the office. John had not spoken to her, and she was grateful. She followed him to the elevators and murmured a quick excuse to part from his company when they reached the office door.

John frowned at her back. She hadn't been able to get away from him quick enough. He hadn't meant to embarrass her or hurt her feelings. But he knew it was better to nip her interest in him now before it grew into something more. He couldn't deny he found her attractive. He also couldn't deny that under other circumstances he'd have kissed her back. He'd have kissed her back and then some. Her trim body and lush mouth were a huge turn on. And in today's blouse, minus the jacket, he'd gotten a good glimpse of her body. Her breasts were fuller than he realized. The suit jackets she wore minimized them. The sheer blouse and camisole she had on today made his mouth water. She had on another skirt, this one pleated, and it swirled around her calves. The heels she wore every day gave a nice shape to her legs and a swing to her hips.

John growled under his breath and headed to the small office Gable had set up for him. It afforded him privacy from the team. He could see Cindy and Melissa at a pair of desks across the aisle from his office. He'd be better off focusing on the job at hand and on the work that needed to be done with his team. And he'd be better off keeping some distance from Isabelle. Melissa could handle most of the daily tasks and coordinate with Isabelle.

John shut the door, but not before he glanced down the hall at Isabelle's desk. She was massaging her temples, and her face was pale. He'd sneaked a few glances at her in the car. While they'd finished up the tour of the warehouse, she'd been flushed but composed. She'd gone back to being businesslike, trying to put the kiss behind her. When they'd stepped outside, she'd checked her phone, then quietly followed him to the car. She'd kept her hood up to hide her face, but he could tell she was pale. Gone was the embarrassed flush. He'd wanted to question her, wondering if she'd gotten some bad news from a vendor or a donor. But she'd been quiet, and he'd let her be.

John dropped into his chair and started up his laptop. First, he needed to send a note to the private investigation firm he used to run background checks. He had the one he'd run on Gable before he'd signed the contract. Nothing alarming was in his background. No one's life was pristine, so he wasn't worried about a few skeletons. But anything involving money, theft, or gambling was bound to set him to worrying. When he found significant financial trouble in a prospective client's past, he would refuse the contract. He also liked to run background checks on employees because sometimes trouble came from others within an organization, not just from the owner or owners.

John sent a list of names and addresses to the agency of all the employees. First, the agency would run everyone's financials. From there, the agency would do a further dive into anyone who looked suspicious. If the financials looked good, they would only dig further upon request. John didn't need a complete history of everyone who worked for The Gables, but anyone with money troubles was always worth investigating further. In a large project like this, it could be easy for someone with the know-how to skim money from the project. He'd seen it happen in the past, and he did his best to minimize the risks to The Heart's Way Foundation.

John was going through some documents when Gable knocked on the door. John waved him in. Gable didn't disturb him much, which he was grateful for. Some clients hovered, while others dumped all the work on him and his team. Gable, thankfully, fell in the middle of those two extremes. Gable was still very invested in the project but had put his faith and trust in him and let him do his job.

Gable took a seat, stretching his long legs out in front of him. "There's a big fundraiser Saturday that I thought you'd like to attend. It's not about the children's hospital, but there will be plenty of people there who are involved in the project."

"What's the fundraiser for?" John tapped a couple of

keys and locked the computer.

"This one is for upgrades to the city's recreational parks. The city doesn't invest much in them; there just aren't funds. The mayor will be there, and several other city officials. There will also be several donors I have worked with in the past, including a couple of board members. We didn't organize this event, but I've been invited. I'll be bringing my wife. Isabelle has an invitation as well, and I thought you'd like to be her plus one."

"Did you ask Isabelle if she wanted to go with me?" After the kiss at the warehouse, Isabelle might not jump at the chance to spend more time with him.

"I mentioned it. She said she'd be happy to escort you." Gable had to convince Isabelle to take John but figured John didn't need to know that.

"No date?" John hadn't intended for that question to pop out of his mouth, but it wasn't exactly a surprise that it slipped out. Knowing he should keep their relationship professional and keeping it that way were two different things.

"No date. No dates at all, that I know of." Gable leaned forward, his forearms resting on his knees. "I know it's none of my business, but I've seen the way you look at her. And I've seen the way she looks at you. She's had a rough couple of years, but she pulled herself up by the bootstraps and got back on track. She hasn't dated since her divorce. And there hasn't been anyone she's been interested in since. But she's interested in you."

John filed away the knowledge that Isabelle was divorced. The fact surprised him. She struck him as a home and hearth type. She also struck him as a faithful, committed type. And the more he got to know her, the more he liked her. He couldn't imagine marrying her and then letting her go. John had never married, preferring his casual relationships to more committed ones. But he didn't doubt he'd eventually get married when he met the right woman. And when he did, he planned on it lasting for life.

"So, what do you say?" Gable rose.

"Sounds like a date. Let Isabelle know she can pick me up at my hotel. Just tell me when."

"I'll have her pick you up at seven. That will give you plenty of time to drive over, find parking, and make your way to the event."

John bid Gable goodnight. Though this wasn't a date, John was looking forward to it. This would allow him to meet the mayor and other potential investors. Rubbing elbows with the city's movers and shakers was always a good idea. John hated small talk, but he'd gotten good at it over the years. It was an essential job skill, one he'd honed. And to be honest, he was looking forward to spending time with Isabelle away from the office. He knew he shouldn't be, but he wasn't going to argue with himself about it. Lying to yourself never solved one's problems.

John knew getting involved with Isabelle was a bad idea. He meant what he'd said to her. He'd been down this road before. Jacqueline had been beautiful and sophisticated. She worked on one of Emmett's other teams. They didn't work much together, but their paths crossed from time to time. One night at a work event, they'd had a few drinks, and against his better judgment, they'd ended up in bed. He'd enjoyed her company, and he'd certainly enjoyed her body. But as was the pattern in most of his relationships, she wanted more from him than he wanted to offer.

She would find her way into his office at odd hours of the day. At first, it didn't bother him. He wasn't opposed to stealing a kiss, and occasionally a little bit more than that, at the office now and again. But then she started making plans for the two of them without consulting him first. She had pouted when he wouldn't accommodate her. At first, she took it in stride, once she stopped pouting. Then she began to get angry with him. She wanted him to drop all his plans to entertain her, and he wasn't willing to put her before his career. She'd made a bunch of ugly accusations the day she broke it off with him, some of which were true. But he wasn't in love with her, and he never would be. She made it impossible to work with her on the rare occasions their jobs crossed after the breakup. Eventually, Emmett gave her a promotion and transferred her to a branch in another state. John had been ready to take the job at the other office himself. He wasn't attached to Los Angeles, and Jacqueline's grief hadn't been worth it. Emmett hadn't wanted him to leave the flagship office and instead moved Jacqueline. Though the promotion was deserved, Jacqueline never caught on as to why she had been moved. John wished her well and was grateful she was out of his hair.

The less rational part of John's brain was telling him that he didn't really work with Isabelle. Neither one of them would have to move or be out of a job when their affair went sour. They weren't coworkers. They were colleagues while they worked on this single project. When the job was over, he'd go back home and forget about her. Of course, it wasn't his brain doing the thinking right now. Isabelle's soft kiss had turned him on. She was so sweet; he'd had the lingering taste of her on his lips from that brief contact the rest of the time they'd spent in the warehouse. He hadn't gone back for the file folders; he'd been too aroused to stay in that confined space with her. Walking around the warehouse hadn't completely cooled him off either. He'd been half aroused the entire drive back to the office.

And here he was making plans to spend Saturday night with her. She'd be out of her office attire. Perhaps she'd wear a slinky, body-hugging dress. He knew she'd have on a pair of heels. Underneath the dress, she would probably have on some pretty sexy underwear. He'd have dozens of excuses to touch her, keeping her close to his side as they mingled.

John cursed under his breath and unlocked his computer. He needed to get to work and stop imagining Isabelle in her underwear. Of course, it was the idea of peeling her out of her underwear that was ruining his focus. When his cell phone rang, John was grateful for the interruption.

Chapter Four

The hotel fundraiser was held on Saturday at one of the most exclusive hotels in town. The hotel was not that far from the mayor's mansion. Security was tight but discreet. John could spot them throughout the room, some mingling in with the guests. Food and champagne were distributed freely. He hadn't left Isabelle's side most of the evening. Right now she was beside him, nibbling on a plate of food. It hadn't escaped his notice that she'd skipped the champagne.

She hadn't disappointed him when she'd picked him up from his hotel. The sapphire blue dress didn't exactly fit her like a glove, but it didn't leave much to the imagination. The neckline was modest, covering up any cleavage that might have worked its way out of a lower bodice, but the dark blue fabric molded her breasts. He had been right; she had been blessed in that part of her anatomy. His fingers itched to touch. The dress fell to the floor in a loose skirt, but when she walked, the fabric molded to what he considered quite a fine backside, as well. The dress had silver threads woven through it, and the light would catch the small threads and shimmer when she moved. She wasn't the flashiest guest in the hotel, but she had his undivided attention.

John also couldn't help but notice Isabelle wasn't talking much. She had looked a little pale under her artfully applied makeup, her body tense. He didn't know if he was the cause of her discomfort, or if something else was. But he knew instinctively something wasn't quite right with her. She smiled and waved at people she knew. She had introduced him to several people, each time stepping slightly behind him as he engaged in conversation. He'd chalk it up to the kiss, but that didn't ring true either. She blushed when she was embarrassed. Her color was not an attractive flush, but a pale translucence.

Isabelle tensed as she sensed John staring at her. Since they arrived, he'd been introduced to most of the people in attendance. He seemed to have quickly lost interest in socializing and had been focused on her ever since. She wasn't sure what he was thinking; no emotions showed on his face. And because she was already tense from the text message she'd received earlier in the day, she could only hope her face wasn't betraying her turmoil.

Isabelle hadn't been surprised to get another vaguely threatening text. Now that she knew her brother was out of prison, and he obviously knew her cell number, she'd been anticipating more messages. This one still wasn't an explicit threat, but she could feel the malice behind the words on the screen. This one made veiled references to her work and ended with the same "see you soon" as the first one. She was sure he knew where she worked, and it was only a matter of time before he found out where she lived. Again, she thought about calling the police, but without concrete proof, it was a waste of time. This message came from a different cell number than the last one, so she couldn't even prove they were from the same person, much less her brother.

Isabelle glanced up from her plate and her eyes met John's. "Aren't you going to eat?"

John nodded but made no move toward the elaborate buffet. Though she had fixed a plate twenty minutes earlier, he noticed she'd eaten very little of it. He'd been nursing a glass of champagne but wasn't hungry. It didn't look like Isabelle was either.

Instead of calling her out on it, he took the plate from her and set it on the tray of a passing waiter. "So, who else should I meet?"

Isabelle was a bit wide-eyed at his taking her plate, but as he probably noticed, she wasn't eating much of it anyway. Instead of arguing with him about his high-handed behavior, she took his arm and led him across the room. She could see Gable was still mingling with his wife and didn't want to interrupt them. But she also spotted Stan and figured if anyone could take her mind off her troubles, it was him.

"I see someone." Isabelle wasn't aware that she'd brought John closer to her side.

John, however, was aware of the brush of Isabelle's body against him. She had a death grip on his arm, her fingers digging a bit into his forearm. The faint perfume smell coming from her skin made his heart beat a little faster. Knowing he needed some distance, he gently released her hold on him as they neared a short, well-manicured man.

Isabelle flushed a bit as John set her away from him, but she kept her composure. She didn't want to embarrass him or herself in front of all these people.

"I was hoping I'd run into you tonight." Stan took Isabelle's hand and kissed her cheek.

Isabelle found her voice and introduced John to Stan. "Stan, this is John Bannon. He's from The Heart's Way, and he's heading up the project."

Stan shook John's hand. "I'm glad I ran into Isabelle, then. I've been hoping to get the chance to meet you. I've heard a lot about the work the foundation does, and it's very impressive. Isabelle has convinced me to part with some of my money toward the project."

John didn't like the somewhat possessive way Stan was holding Isabelle's hand. Though not very tall, the man was taller than Isabelle. He supposed women found him attractive. He looked fit and healthy, despite the silver hair and obvious signs of age around his eyes. He was probably old enough to be Isabelle's father, but she wasn't looking at him in a familial way. He wasn't sure what was going on behind Isabelle's violet eyes, but it was obvious the pair were quite friendly.

But despite the spark of jealousy John felt, he found himself enjoying Stan's company. He had released Isabelle's hand, and she once again stood next to him. Stan was quite the storyteller and easily kept the conversation flowing between them.

"So how did the two of you meet?" John saw Isabelle tense up when he asked the question.

"We were both volunteering at a shelter downtown.

That was before she went to work for Gable. I was thinking about hiring her myself right before Gable stole her away."

Isabelle laughed a little at that and relaxed. Stan was aware she was sensitive about the circumstances surrounding her stay at the shelter. "You certainly don't need my help. Your secretary is the most capable woman I've ever met."

Stan laughed at that, and Isabelle was glad the awkward question had been answered.

"Yes, but you can never have enough good help, can you?" Stan's eyes strayed behind Isabelle. "Looks like Gable's looking for me. I'd better go say hello. It was nice meeting you."

John took the hand Stan offered, still surprised he'd enjoyed the man's company. Though he looked like one of the city's elite, he was very down-to-earth.

"How much money did you get him to part with?" John took Isabelle's hand, leading her around the room toward the open balcony doors. Though it was cool outside, the inside of the hotel banquet hall was getting a bit stuffy.

Isabelle smiled and rattled off a number. "He was extremely generous with his money, considering the money he's losing by renting us that warehouse so cheap. But Stan says he has more money than he can ever use, and he might as well put it to good use."

The amount surprised John, who had figured the amount would have been nominal. "I guess so. And he volunteers at a shelter?"

"He says money is all fine and good, but it's people and their time the shelter really needs. He says money is easy."

Isabelle shrugged. "I don't have a lot of money to donate, so giving a little bit of my time once or twice a month isn't that big a sacrifice. Though, with this project going on, I let the staff know I wouldn't be around for a while. But Stan still goes in once a week, so I don't feel quite so bad."

John nodded at that. Both of them would have very little free time over the next month or so. Once construction began, the workload would lessen for a while. Then once construction was completed, they once again would be just as busy, if not more so, than they were now.

Isabelle let John lead her outside. The sky was clear, but there was still a chill in the air. The temperature had gone up a few degrees, but spring hadn't quite settled in yet. But the cold air felt good on her overheated cheeks, and it helped with some of her tension. The stars were bright despite the ambient light, and she lifted her face to the sky.

The pair was quiet for a while as they simply absorbed the night air. Isabelle hated to break the peace between them, but she was getting chilled. "I should probably take you back to Gable. You still haven't met the mayor."

John took Isabelle's hand but didn't move them back inside. Instead, he looked down at her hand, her nails adorned with nothing but a clear polish. John wanted to kiss her but reminded himself again that it was a bad idea. Once he got a real taste of her, he knew it wouldn't end with just a kiss.

Isabelle's breath hitched as John held her hand. Her breath stopped when his eyes found hers. Remembering how he had rejected her in the warehouse office, she slipped her hand from his and turned away from him. She thought she read desire in his eyes, a desire she knew was in her own, but she had no illusions that he would act on his impulses.

Isabelle didn't speak again until she found Gable. She turned John over to him and excused herself. She needed to step away from him and regain her balance. Her strong reaction to him still caught her by surprise sometimes. His thumb had been stroking the top of her hand, and even that simple touch made her flustered.

A half-hour later, she saw John with Gable and the mayor. She didn't see Gable's wife, but Caitlyn knew everyone here tonight and most likely found some friends. She let another half an hour pass before she made her way back to John and Gable.

John's eyes met hers. "Ready to go?"

Isabelle nodded, unable to speak past the lump in her throat. They had already been here for over three hours. Her feet hurt, her head hurt, and she wanted nothing more than to go home and pull the blankets over her head.

John took their coat tickets and fetched them. Isabelle bid Gable goodnight, hugging Caitlyn, who had made her way back to her husband's side.

Caitlyn spoke to the pair. "We'll have to have you over soon. It's been too long since you've joined us for dinner."

"I'd love to." Isabelle answered before turning to John. "You need to try Caitlyn's cooking. It's amazing. She should have been a professional chef."

"I wouldn't go that far, but I certainly enjoy cooking. Gable keeps saying we could hire a cook, but I won't have it. And if he's honest, he doesn't mean it."

Gable kissed his wife affectionately. "I would if it made you happy. But I'd be secretly unhappy eating someone else's cooking."

Isabelle smiled at the teasing, her mind off her problems for the moment. "Goodnight, and we'll see you soon."

Isabelle let John help her with her coat and enjoyed the feel of his hand on her back as he led her toward the valet. She once again absorbed the night, knowing that the feeling of happiness wouldn't last.

John wanted to kiss the smile on Isabelle's lips but held himself back. He concentrated on the night instead. He had decided to rent a car instead of relying on Gable or Isabelle to fetch him. He'd met Isabelle at his hotel but had led her to his car.

Isabelle thanked John as he helped her into the car, lightly closing the door behind him. She had taken a cab to the hotel, but John had gotten angry earlier in the evening when she told him she would grab a cab home from the hotel. He'd gotten pretty close to losing his temper over it, so she had relented. She quietly directed John to her apartment building, feeling slightly uncomfortable because it wasn't in the best neighborhood. She knew she shouldn't feel ashamed because she couldn't afford something nicer. Though Gable paid her well, she still worked for a not-for-profit organization, and she didn't make as much money as she would have made doing the same job elsewhere.

Isabelle guided John to the parking area of her apartment building. It was rare to have parking, and the lot was one of the reasons she'd chosen this particular building.

She was going to let herself out when John stopped her. She watched as he rounded the car and opened her door. Uncomfortable now that they were at her building, she nervously took the hand he held out.

"You don't have to walk me up."

John grunted at that and kept her hand in his. "It's almost midnight. There's no way I'm letting you walk to your apartment by yourself."

She tried to pretend disinterest in his presence and guided him to her door. Her apartment was on the second floor, and she liked to take the stairs. She led him to the staircase and her door. Torn, but not wanting to be rude, she unlocked her door and faced him.

"Do you want to come in for a minute?"

John was mildly shocked by the invitation. He had bet she'd close the door in his face as soon as she was inside after the argument she'd given him earlier about driving her home. He simply entered the apartment without answering her.

Isabelle gestured him to her loveseat. The apartment was too small for a couch, so she'd opted for a loveseat and a pair of chairs. She had a television, but she kept it hidden in a cabinet. The television was a recent purchase, one she'd made at Christmas when it was on sale. Slowly but surely, she was filling up the space. After being homeless, she was overly cautious about spending money on things that were not necessities. She didn't have television service; she opted to stream free shows instead.

"Nice and cozy." John leaned back on the loveseat, watching Isabelle stare off at the far wall.

John's voice brought her back to the moment. "I don't need much space. And goodness knows, I'm not here much anyway. I don't have anything to offer you besides water. It's a little late for coffee. I'll be up all night."

John shook his head. "I'm good. I had enough at the fundraiser. The mayor had a lot of nice things to say about you."

Isabelle could smile at that. Never in her lifetime did she ever expect to get involved in politics, even peripherally. "He attends a lot of our fundraisers. Just having his name on the guest list is enough to get several businessmen and other politicians to our events. For a politician, he's really nice."

"Don't like politics?" John took her hand since she was standing beside the loveseat and pulled her onto the cushion next to him.

"Not really. My dad was heavily into politics. Mostly he liked having people with power in his pocket."

John digested that bit of information. "Doesn't sound like you care for your father."

Isabelle swallowed the lump that formed in her throat. She hadn't meant to mention her father. But of course, he couldn't know she was talking about the man who'd gotten his father fired from his job all those years ago. "Let's just say we never saw eye to eye. He was a hard man to like."

"Was?" John took her hand. Her fingers were trembling. He hoped he was the reason for the tremors and not her father.

She nodded. "I can't say anyone missed him when he was gone. My mother certainly didn't, other than missing the money he earned. They fought often, but as long as she could buy the things she desired, she didn't much care what he did."

John turned her hand over, stroking his thumb on her palm. He felt her pulse leap when his fingers brushed over the pulse in her wrist. Her eyes dilated, and her lips parted. "You make me want to forget the rules."

Isabelle wasn't sure how they jumped from the topic of her father to her obvious attraction to him. He was looking at her mouth now, his thumb stroking her wrist. "What rules?"

John smiled, lifting the forefinger of his free hand to her lips. "The ones that say getting involved is a bad idea."

Isabelle's voice was breathy when she spoke. "Right. Those rules. Are you saying you want to break them?"

John ignored her question, instead lifting her hand to his mouth. He pressed a kiss to her wrist, but that was all he allowed.

Isabelle hadn't known the skin on her wrist was so sensitive. He kissed her wrist again, then her palm. She could do nothing else but look into his eyes. They'd darkened, and she was sure she saw raw desire in them. She lifted her other palm to his cheek but pulled it back when he turned away from her. She was disheartened when he dropped her hand and rose.

"Like I said, it's a bad idea."

Utterly confused by his actions, Isabelle rose to face him. She wasn't sure where the boldness came from, but she had to ask the questions that popped out of her mouth. "Are you attracted to me? Or did you pull away because you're not really attracted to me, and you just got caught up in the moment?"

"I'd have to be dead not to be attracted to you. You're an incredibly beautiful woman, Isabelle. But attraction can be set aside. It's about being an adult and not acting on your impulses." John headed for the door. He couldn't help but notice that she slept on a twin mattress. He guessed she didn't invite men over.

John left Isabelle staring after him. She dropped back onto the loveseat, lowering her head to her hands. She didn't understand her consuming attraction to John. He couldn't make it any plainer that though he liked the way she looked, he just wasn't interested. But the deep ache in the pit of her belly didn't want to be ignored.

Isabelle moaned and wrapped her arms around her waist. Why couldn't she have found herself attracted to any of the dozens of men she'd met over the past year? The men she met were successful. They had good jobs, drove nice cars, and were flashy dressers. But they hadn't appealed to her. After her divorce, she had wondered if she'd ever be attracted to a man again. The giddy sensation she felt around John reminded her of how she felt about her boyfriend in high school.

She had met Danny when she was fourteen, a year after John had left town. He had been her first and her last crush. They had dated until she was eighteen. He'd been her first lover, and they'd played at being in love their last year together. Then he'd gone away to college and never looked back. She'd ended up marrying her father's business partner a year later. She hadn't been in love with Nathan, and he hadn't cared. He wanted a young wife, one he could show off to his friends, and one that was socially acceptable. She needed someone to help take care of her and her mother, who was useless after her father's death. Her brother certainly hadn't helped. And after Danny broke up with her, she hadn't cared much who she married. Marrying Nathan seemed like the perfect solution to her problems. He was good-looking, and though older than her, not old enough to be her father. And for a couple of years, their deal had worked.

But neither Danny nor Nathan made her ache this way. Her hands ached to touch. Her mouth ached to kiss him. And the rest of her simply ached for his body against hers.

"Get over it, girl." Isabelle hoped the words spoken out loud would help. Certainly, pining over John wasn't doing anyone any good. And she was only going to embarrass herself further if she kept it up.

Isabelle's musings were interrupted by her cell phone. The loud ping had her heart racing. Her fingers, trembling this time with anxiety, picked up the phone.

The message this time simply said, "New boyfriend?"

Isabelle dropped the phone, rushing to the windows. She didn't see anyone below, no shadows where someone could hide. She pulled the curtains closed and shut off the lamp. She double-checked the locks before going back to her phone. This time she sent a message back.

"Why are you doing this?" Isabelle tried to slow down her breathing while she waited for an answer.

"You don't deserve to be happy. Sleep tight."

Isabelle curled up on her bed, fully dressed. She didn't

think she'd sleep a wink. She was right.

Chapter Five

John hadn't thought it possible, but Isabelle was even paler Monday morning than she'd been during the fundraiser. It looked like she'd tried to cover up the purple bruises under her eyes. He saw Gable looking at her concernedly, but the man didn't make a move to talk to her. Something was going on with Isabelle, and he knew it was something besides his rejecting her for the second time. He wasn't so egotistical as to believe she'd spent Saturday and Sunday night pining away for him.

John decided to talk to Gable. "What's up with your project coordinator? She looks like death warmed over this morning."

Gable, not wanting to break any confidences, gave him the excuse Isabelle had given him. "She said she wasn't feeling well this weekend and didn't sleep much. Something about a stomach ache."

"And you bought that story? She was fine when I dropped her off Saturday night." John glanced over to Isabelle's desk. She was on the phone and didn't notice she was the topic of their conversation.

"Isabelle's not a liar. Why, do you know something I don't?" Despite not wanting to betray her trust, Gable wasn't opposed to fishing for answers.

"Nope. I thought maybe she was upset with me about her wanting me to, but not kissing her on Saturday night."

Gable sputtered a bit, not sure what to say to John's frank statement. He opted to be just as candid. "Why didn't you? She likes you."

"We work together, and romances and work don't mix. I'd better get to work. I've got some phone calls to make this morning." John left Gable staring after him and went into his office. The small room had a door and offered some privacy. He needed it for the calls he was going to make.

Something about Isabelle wasn't sitting well with him. Despite the feeling of familiarity, he didn't quite trust this sudden attraction she seemed to have toward him. And if he guessed right, she hadn't been sleeping well since she'd kissed him at the warehouse. He didn't like coincidences, and her sudden interest in him, paired with her obvious anxiety, made him wonder if the two things were related.

The first thing he did was send an email to the investigation company he used for background checks. It was still early for them to be open on the West Coast, but he knew someone would return his email after they finished the cursory background checks on the list of names he emailed them. He'd been putting the email off, half afraid something would come back about Isabelle. He imagined she was as squeaky clean as she appeared, but he'd been fooled before. And her odd behavior set off his warning alarms.

A couple of hours later, John glanced down at the number on his cell phone and rose to shut the door so he wouldn't be overheard. He'd been watching Isabelle and Cindy go over some paperwork while he sent some emails out to vendors. "Hi, Jack."

Jack Warner was one of the investigators at the agency. Generally, John preferred Jack, and since the foundation sent a lot of money the agency's way, he usually got what he wanted. Jack was also a good friend.

Jack got down to business. "Most everything is routine. You've got a few employees overextended on their credit cards, and one guy has two mortgages."

John focused on the word 'most.' "Who is standing out?"

"I'm not entirely sure. You've got a woman there with a really shaky financial past. Her name is Isabelle Masterson. Up until her job at the foundation last year, her bank account was pretty much zero at the end of every month. She had no credit cards under her name, though she has one now with a small balance. I did a quick search and there is something fishy about her. Looks like she got divorced six years ago. And it looks like there was no money from a divorce settlement and no alimony. There are no children, and it looks like they made a clean split. She moved out of the condo she and her ex-husband owned and into a different apartment. She quit one job and then was fired from another. Then her apartment manager evicted her. After that, up until a year ago, she had no address. Her last address before her current address belongs to a man named Stan Oakley. Then she bailed on him and moved into her current apartment. It's in a low-income neighborhood. She now has a savings account and pays her bills on time."

John absorbed what Jack was saying, his eyes straying to Isabelle. He recognized the name Stan Oakley as the man he had met at the fundraiser. The man Isabelle obviously was more than friends with. He wondered if she had gotten him to agree to sign the lease on the warehouse before or after she moved in with him. "You have no idea where she lived before she moved in with Stan?"

"No. She wasn't cashing a paycheck; I can tell you that much. The only money coming in was a small amount of unemployment, and that ran out fast."

"See what else you can find." John hung up the phone and leaned back in his seat. Stan Oakley was old enough to be her father. From all accounts, he was very active in the community and the city's social scene. John had Jack check out Stan and his business as soon as the name was mentioned to him. He seemed on the up and up, and he'd enjoyed the man's company when they'd met. They were finishing up the lease agreement, and The Gables would be locked into a five-year agreement.

It was none of his business if Isabelle had been having an affair with Stan. It wasn't any of his business if she still was, though if she was, then her coming onto him was a red flag. He was still surprised she was divorced. There was something innocent about her, with her smiles and blushes. John couldn't help but wonder if it was all an act. And if it was, what was she hiding?

It also seemed a little circumspect that she just happened to be living with the man who gave Gable a great deal on a warehouse. Was there an ulterior motive? Gable hadn't mentioned a personal relationship between the pair, only that they had met volunteering at a shelter. Did they use volunteering as a way to work their way into foundations like The Gables and steal money? John had a sudden urge to see the books at the warehouse. When he and Isabelle had been in the office, she had kissed him. Was that a distraction? He'd left the office without examining any of the documentation in the file folders. Was that her plan all along?

John hated being so suspicious, but with his military training and the years he'd spent working with various people claiming to be committed to a charity who weren't, he couldn't help but wonder. Isabelle could be as innocent as she seemed. Or she and Stan could be involved in a bigger scam. Stan, as the property owner, had access to the building. Very few people did things simply out of the kindness of their hearts. And Stan was taking quite a loss on the rent for the building.

John spent the rest of the day trying to concentrate on work. By four o'clock, he couldn't stand being cooped up any longer. John grabbed his coat and tucked his cell phone in his pocket. He didn't need his laptop, but he might need to snap a few pictures. John didn't want to believe Isabelle could be scamming Gable. But he was too attracted to her to be unbiased. Proof of innocence was what he needed. And though he was paying Jack to investigate her past, he wanted to check the financials at the warehouse himself.

Isabelle watched John as he brushed past her and Cindy without saying a word. She hadn't said anything to him this morning, and she hadn't had an opportunity to talk to him the rest of the day. She was avoiding him, not that he seemed to notice or care. Gable hadn't mentioned her making googly eyes again, but she knew she still was. Her gaze kept glancing toward the closed door of his office. Apparently, she couldn't help herself, even now after he'd left her Saturday night with his mouth on her wrist and palm a tangible memory.

Other women watched him, so at least she didn't completely stand out. Not that she blamed them. Even Cindy, who had worked with him for the past couple of years, stared after him. The problem was she knew the women watching him were also watching her watch him, and that was just as embarrassing as the pass she'd made. The whole office knew she was smitten. She sighed as the main office door closed behind him. In an hour or so, she could head out and get a reprieve from the sight of John. She turned her attention back to Cindy and hoped she could get her feelings under control. She also hoped John had left for the evening. She didn't want to face him again today.

It wasn't like she didn't have other problems besides John. Since Saturday night she'd gotten a dozen texts from a couple of different phones. The messages before Saturday night were non-incriminating. But after Saturday, they didn't stay that way. Her brother threatened her that he'd get her fired again. He threatened John with vague threats as he referred to him as "her boyfriend." Then later Sunday he'd threatened John by name. It occurred to her that at some point on Sunday, Marcus remembered John from when they were teenagers. Knowing it was John coming out of her apartment must have angered him further. Now he was just being nasty. She still couldn't prove it was

Marcus on the other end of the text messages, so she still had nothing to go to the police with.

She was tempted to turn off her phone, but that wouldn't stop the messages from coming in. She thought about changing her phone number, but the phone was a work phone, not a personal one, and coworkers and clients had the number. She could only hope he'd get bored with the taunts or slip up and reveal who he was. Isabelle knew Marcus wasn't stupid, but perhaps he'd give enough away to incriminate himself.

On top of all that, she was feeling guilty. Gable had asked her if anything was wrong, and she'd told him she had a stomachache. And though that was technically true, she'd neglected to tell Gable why her stomach hurt. She didn't want Gable trying to find and confront her brother, so she'd lied to him.

The hour passed without John's return. She let out a sigh of relief and packed up her stuff for the night. Isabelle was afraid to go home. But it wasn't as if she had much choice. Hitching her bag to her shoulder and gathering her courage, she headed to her car.

Isabelle made it to her car, then her apartment, without incident. She was halfway through fixing her dinner when her cell phone pinged. Unable not to look, she crossed the small apartment and picked up her phone. What she saw chilled her blood. Without thought or reason, Isabelle grabbed her purse, tossed her phone inside, and headed to the warehouse where the photo on her phone from John's phone showed him unconscious on the floor, lying amid a pile of glass and rubble.

* * *

The warehouse lights were off; only the lamps from the street lit the parking lot. John looked but didn't see the guard. So much for security. It was only five o'clock, but no one was around. John walked over to the security booth, but it too was empty. He didn't see any cars in the parking lot. It wouldn't surprise him if the guard kicked off early since it was rare for anyone to come around after hours.

John parked the rental car beside the warehouse and worked his way to the main entrance. He cursed when he saw the alarm light was off. The guard hadn't even bothered to lock up before he left. The door swung open easily, but there were no lights on in the building. He hit the main switches, illuminating the space. His curses grew louder.

Half the contents of the warehouse were destroyed. Drywall had been sliced, glass had been smashed, and small boxes of screws and nails were strewn about. There was a water puddle under the lumber and drywall where someone had stuffed up the utility sinks along the back wall and turned the faucets on full blast. Furniture was smashed in the back room, and the file room had been tossed. The further in he got, he saw someone had also lit a fire. Some of the wood had burned but not much. For the most part, the wood was chemically treated and didn't burn as fast. He'd smelled smoke when he'd entered the warehouse but hadn't seen any signs of fire until now.

John stood quietly, trying to hear if anyone was still in

the warehouse. This wouldn't be the first, and certainly wouldn't be the last time that a warehouse had been vandalized in this neighborhood. What bothered him was that nothing looked missing. It just looked destroyed. On construction sites, pipes and wiring tended to disappear and then reappear when sold for scrap. But that didn't seem to be the case.

John walked carefully across the glass, cautious that he was wearing dress shoes and not work boots. He didn't hear anything at first but picked up a length of pipe that was lying nearby, just in case. As he made his way through the warehouse, he heard a tinkle of glass, then nothing. He went to the utility sinks and shut off the faucets. Remaining still and alert, he waited for the sound to come again. After a few moments of nothing, he started back toward the office space. Nothing looked ruined in there; it just looked tossed.

The first man rushed him from behind, and John spun, catching the guy off guard as he struck him from the side instead of full-on. The second man came from behind a stack of lumber, a length of it in his hand. John managed to block a blow from the assailant and got a solid hit in. A third man caught him next to his temple with a board, and John went down. He felt himself start to lose consciousness and felt trickles of blood dripping from his forehead.

The first kick hit him right in the kidney. The second from the front hit his solar plexus. After that, John wasn't sure where they hit him, just that they did. John tried to fight, but the three men subdued him, holding him down. He felt only a few more kicks before he passed out completely.

* * *

The warehouse was in shambles. Lumber had been set on fire, water from the overflowing sinks had soaked the insulation and lumber, and drywall had been busted up. Isabelle hardly saw any of it. She frantically searched the destruction for any sign of John. The text message and photo that showed John lying amid the destruction were on her phone. She tried to see if anything in the picture resembled the space around her. A bit of graffiti grabbed her attention, and Isabelle ran as fast as she could in her heels to the other side of the warehouse. There she found John.

She dropped to her knees, her tights tearing as she knelt in the broken glass beside John. She wasn't aware of the glass that sliced up her knees and embedded in her skin. He was breathing, but he wasn't awake. There wasn't much blood, but there was a gash in the front of his forehead, his hair matted where the blood had dripped and was now drying. She didn't see any other signs of injury, but she couldn't see much of him under his coat. She pulled the decorative scarf from around her neck and tried to staunch the blood oozing from the wound. John moaned, and Isabelle wept in relief.

"John? John, can you hear me?" Isabelle lay beside him, trying to see if he was opening his eyes. She didn't want to move him, but she couldn't see his face without lying beside him.

John heard a soft voice calling to him, the sound

familiar. He opened his eyes to see pretty violet eyes behind a pair of glasses gazing into his. A vision from the past overlaid the present. "Izzy?"

She smiled at him, sniffling and wiping her tears. "Yes, John, it's Izzy. Lie still."

The sound of voices had her rising to her feet. She saw the paramedics and waved them over. She stepped back from them. She'd called 911 on the way to the warehouse, once she had begun thinking straight. It took a few minutes before the paramedics felt comfortable moving him. They strapped him to a board as a precaution, and Isabelle took his hand as the men wheeled him outside to the ambulance. She sat in the ambulance out of the way. The paramedics were doing some cognitive exercises and trying to assess his injuries. When they cut his shirt from him, she saw dark bruises forming on his ribs and around his back. If she had to guess, she'd bet he'd been kicked in the ribs and kidneys repeatedly.

Isabelle was hardly aware of the tears that were trickling down her cheeks. Her brother had done this to him. It wasn't enough that he punish her. He wanted to punish everyone around her. The fact that this was John had probably given her brother endless pleasure. He'd not only attacked his sister, but he'd also attacked an old nemesis.

It was two hours before she was allowed to see him. In that time, the emergency room team had cleaned up the cuts on her hands and knees. A particularly bad cut on her leg needed stitches. She submitted to them, and the tetanus shot, feeling displaced. All she wanted was to see John. She wasn't sure if he would remember anything when he came to, but she wanted him to. When he'd called her Izzy, she'd felt her heart swell that he finally remembered. The other part of her was worried he'd be angry with her for her deceit.

Her stomach was in knots when she was finally allowed to see him. He was sitting propped up on the hospital bed, the lights off, and an ice pack pressed against the front of his head.

Isabelle shut the curtains behind her. Her voice was low when she spoke. "How are you feeling? The doctor said they're going to keep you overnight."

John massaged his temple. "I've got a killer headache, and I feel like I've been kicked in the gut."

Isabelle set her purse down and pulled the chair closer to him. But instead of sitting down, she brushed her fingers across his brow. He had a few cuts on his face from lying in the glass she'd sliced her knees on. Tears welled up in her eyes, guilt heavy on her heart. "I'm so sorry, John."

He looked at her through slitted eyes, the faint light from the outer room making his headache worse. "Why would you be sorry? This isn't your fault."

"That's where you're wrong. I know who did this to you and it's all my fault. He wouldn't be here if it weren't for me. He wouldn't have done this if I had left."

John set the ice pack down and took her chin in his hands. "Who did this?"

Her voice was low when she answered him. "My brother. He did this."

A memory from the warehouse came back to him. His

fingers tightened on her chin. "Izzy. I remembered. You're Izzy Douglas. Your brother is Marcus Douglas."

He released her chin and swore. "It's been driving me crazy. Something about you was so familiar, but I was certain we never met. But we did. We met the night your brother jumped me after school and landed me in the hospital. He and his friends dragged me out to the football field behind the school and beat the tar out of me. You're the one who found me and called the cops."

"He'd been bragging about it with his friends. I rode my bike to the school to find you. Then I rode to the police station."

"After you covered me with a blanket and left me with a hot thermos of coffee."

She gave him a watery laugh. "It was cold, and I couldn't think of anything else to bring. I snuck out to find you." She didn't add the beating she'd gotten when her dad found out she'd snuck out. He'd accused her of all sorts of filthy things when she'd refused to tell him where she'd gone. It had taken two days before she could sit down without wincing. But the bruises on her back and backside hadn't stopped her from coming to the hospital to visit him. He'd spent two weeks there. She'd visited him every day. He hadn't been happy about her visits, but he'd tolerated them. In her mind, it was the least she could do to make up to him for what her brother had done. It wouldn't be the last time she tried to atone for his deviant behavior.

John took her hands, toying with her fingers. He had mixed emotions about who she was. Her brother had been a borderline sociopath. His father bailed him out of trouble time and again. John's parents pressed charges, and that time Malcolm Douglas hadn't been able to buy his son out of trouble. Marcus had spent some time in a juvenile detention center because of that incident. John knew he hadn't spent much time there, thanks to his father's influence, but at least he'd been punished.

"I can't believe you're little Izzy." John dropped her fingers and once again massaged his forehead.

"I'll do that." Isabelle sat on the bed and scooted forward so she could massage his temples.

Despite his mixed feelings at the moment, her fingers were magic on his aching head. He bit back a moan. "So why do you think your brother did this?"

"Because he told me he did. He warned me that I'd better stay away from you. He told me I'd be sorry if I didn't. Earlier this evening, I got a text message from your phone with a picture of you unconscious at the warehouse. I called the paramedics before I left to find you. I beat them by about five minutes."

John stilled her fingers. "You're telling me you came to the warehouse knowing your brother had been there? Are you out of your mind?"

"I had to come. You were hurt." She tried to free her hand, but he refused to let her fingers go.

"No. What you should have done is call the police and stayed put. What if he had been waiting for you? He could have hurt you." John tugged her closer.

Isabelle flinched as his fingers crushed hers. She was relieved when he let her fingers go. She realized he saw the bandage on her palm. Then his fingers trailed to the hem of her skirt. He lifted the hem and saw the bandages she had on her knees.

"What happened?" His eyes roamed over the rest of her, looking for any other injuries. "Did he hurt you?"

"No, he wasn't there. No one was there when I got there. He's not stupid enough to hang around the crime scene. I cut my knees on the broken glass you were lying on. That's how you got those cuts on your face."

John rubbed his fingertips on her bare thigh above the bandage, her tights long since discarded. "You could have been seriously hurt. Don't you ever do that again. I can take care of myself."

She raised her eyes to his and was not surprised by the anger in them. Her voice was barely a whisper. "I'm sorry."

John cupped her face again. He was angry with her, but he also had a desire to kiss her. Had they been anywhere else, had he been in more control of his impulses, he would have backed away. But her cheeks were streaked with tears, tears she'd cried for him, and his resistance faded.

Isabelle knew what he intended, and all she could do was watch him as he bent his head to hers. When his lips met hers, she clutched his shoulders. His kiss was rough, his lingering anger with her evident in the kiss. She didn't resist his kiss, nor did she resist him when his tongue insisted on entrance to her mouth. She moaned when he deepened the kiss, her fingers now digging into his shoulders.

John lifted his head for a moment to catch his breath. The kiss had started in anger, but he wasn't feeling angry anymore. He bent his head again; this time his lips were teasing and coaxing hers. He pulled her closer, his tongue tracing her lips, savoring her mouth instead of bruising it.

"I see you're feeling better." The doctor chuckled as the pair broke hastily apart.

John glared at him. "I feel like I've been hit in the head with a brick."

"It could very well have been a brick. It's hard to say, but I doubt it. A brick would have done more damage. I'm guessing a two-by-four, or some other piece of lumber lying around the warehouse."

Isabelle slipped off the bed and into the chair she had pulled over. She felt the heat of embarrassment on her cheeks, but the doctor didn't seem to notice. He finished his exam and told them he was just waiting for transport to take John to his room. He needed to be monitored. He had a concussion, bruised ribs, and an assortment of cuts from the glass, and bruises where he'd fallen and been kicked. Thankfully nothing was broken.

"You'll be fine, but we need to be sure. The police are waiting outside the room. I'll send them in."

John nodded. He saw Isabelle tense, but otherwise, she maintained her composure.

Isabelle sat in silence as John relayed his version of the story to the police. She showed them the photo on her phone, knowing it wasn't much good as evidence since it had been sent from John's phone. John's phone was missing, so they couldn't dust it for fingerprints. What she couldn't believe was that John was not telling the cops it was her brother who had sent the picture. Instead of enlightening them, she sat quietly. She answered the questions they had but didn't contribute more than to answer their direct questions.

John felt Isabelle's questioning eyes on him, but he didn't look at her. There was no proof that her brother did this. Even if the cops picked him up for questioning, they'd release him. There was nothing to hold him on except Isabelle's accusations. And if the police started questioning Marcus, they would also direct their questions to Isabelle. The cops would start digging into Isabelle's life. John wasn't ready to let them start doing that until he had answers to his questions. Isabelle had kept her identity a secret from him. He wanted to find out why.

John wasn't sure what was going on, or why Marcus had sought him out instead of Isabelle. Until he had the facts and proof, he was keeping what Isabelle had told him to himself. If the cops picked up Marcus for questioning, it would just anger him more, and that could come back on Isabelle. So until John was sure he could keep Isabelle safe from her brother, he wasn't going to share her suspicions.

The cops left, and John could tell they weren't holding their breath, hoping to catch the guys who did this. As far as the cops were concerned, John had interrupted a theft. With so many construction projects going on around the city, vandalism of the sites was commonplace. Catching and prosecuting them was practically impossible, especially when they weren't caught on camera.

It was another hour before he was settled into a room. Isabelle had closed her eyes while waiting for his room, and he let her be. He didn't want to question her with an audience outside the curtains and was in no shape to pick up where they had left off, assuming she'd be willing.

While the nurse helped him settle in the bed, she paced the room. When the nurse left, Isabelle turned to John. "Should we call Gable?"

John groaned in relief as the throbbing in his head lessened. "Not tonight. There's nothing he can do right now. We'll tell him in the morning."

She nodded. "I'll have to call the insurance company and get a claim started. The vandals destroyed thousands of dollars' worth of materials. It will set the project back."

"I think we should concentrate on your brother and why you think he did this."

Isabelle's pacing increased. "It's a long story, and you're in no shape to hear it right now. You need to rest."

John wasn't up to arguing with her. What little energy he had earlier was fading fast. "I'll rest if you promise to stay here with me tonight."

She paused her pacing. She wanted to stay with him but hadn't wanted to push. She remembered when he'd been eighteen. He'd yelled and argued, trying to throw her out of his room. He'd even threatened to have the nurse remove her. But he'd eventually relented and let her stay. She'd only been thirteen at the time. She was sure he took pity on her when he'd decided to let her stay because she had begun to cry. This time she had been mentally preparing herself for a battle over her staying with him tonight. His capitulation was surprising, but she wasn't going to question it. She made up the pull-out bed designed for visitors.

John relaxed when she finally laid down. He'd been

afraid she'd leave. If her brother had done this, it was possible he'd be lying in wait for her to come home. His stomach knotted with the vision of her bloody and beaten, lying alone in her apartment. At least if she was here, she was safe. John drifted to sleep with the remembered taste of Isabelle on his lips.

Isabelle lay there for a while, thinking about John and the past. She knew she needed to tell John the truth about her brother and her family. Because that wasn't conducive to sleep, she instead thought about John's kiss. Thinking about the kiss wasn't making her sleepy either, but it was better than thinking about her brother.

John's kiss had been everything she had dreamed of and more. She was a grown woman. She'd been married. She'd had one lover before her husband, though they'd been teenagers. Neither of them had ever kissed her like that, as if he could swallow her whole. No man she had ever met had kissed her like that. John made number three. Perhaps the third time was the charm. Isabelle smiled to herself at the silly thought and rolled over to get comfortable. She needed to sleep. She sighed and snuggled down. She drifted off to sleep thinking about John.

Chapter Six

"I still can't believe you're Izzy Douglas. Why didn't you tell me when we met?" John sipped his coffee while propped up in the bed. His head was still throbbing but not with the same intensity as the night before. The nurses had woken him every couple of hours, and despite the lack of sleep, he was feeling wide awake. This last time they'd woken him, his mind had kicked into high gear and made sleep impossible. And every time they woke him up, Isabelle woke up with him. He could see dark circles under her eyes but figured she probably looked a sight better than he did. The cuts on his face were irritating and starting to itch, and he imagined he had dark circles under his eyes that had nothing to do with a lack of sleep.

"It felt odd to say something. We weren't exactly friends fifteen years ago. And when you didn't recognize me, I thought it best to leave it alone." Isabelle was sipping an apple juice, foregoing coffee. She didn't need the added stimulation. She was still jittery from the night's events.

"I should have recognized those eyes. When you were a kid, it was your eyes that made me relent and let you stay. Such sad, pretty eyes."

Isabelle shifted uncomfortably under his gaze. There was a new warmth in them that hadn't been there before.

She didn't know if it was because he now knew who she was, or if it was because he'd kissed her. "Maybe it's because my eyes are not sad anymore."

"I saw fear, concern, and sadness in your eyes last night. I think it's time you told me what happened."

Isabelle could hear voices and various noises in the halls. "I think we should wait until I get you back to your hotel room. Then we need to tell Gable what happened. What I need to tell you is personal, and I don't want someone to overhear me."

"All right. We can talk about it later." John leaned back and closed his eyes. Despite not feeling tired, he started to drift off when he felt Isabelle kiss his forehead.

"I'm going to go get my car so I can drive you back to your hotel later. And I need to take a shower and change my clothes. If you let me have your key, I can get you a change of clothes."

"It's in my wallet, inside my jacket. Your brother took my phone but not my wallet. I guess I should be grateful."

Isabelle handed the wallet to John to let him fish out the key. She put it in her purse and brushed the hair back from his forehead. "I'll be back soon."

John closed his eyes again, but sleep was eluding him. He couldn't imagine what she wanted to tell him that was so personal she didn't want anyone overhearing her. But then again, this was Marcus they were talking about. He hadn't seen Marcus since his court appearance fifteen years ago. As a teenager, Marcus had been tall, taller than John. He'd worked out obsessively. John had first met him at the local gym. They both spent a lot of time working out there. For reasons John never understood, Marcus had taken an instant dislike to him.

John also knew him from school. John was not a fan of the Douglas clan. Malcolm Douglas owned a local construction company that did a lot of work for the state. John had worked with his dad for a few summers for Douglas Construction. Then when John was seventeen, his dad was fired. His dad had found out Douglas Construction was cutting corners. He threatened to turn them in. In the end, nothing came of the claims because Malcolm had bought off the inspectors who had certified the work. His dad was fired, and then he was fired immediately thereafter. With both him and his dad out of work, things had been tough.

John had wanted nothing to do with Izzy Douglas when she came that first day to visit him. John knew full well who had attacked him. He recognized Marcus and his friends. Izzy had overheard her brother and come to his rescue. Izzy had visited him that first day, carrying a handful of spring flowers she'd picked on her way to visit him. She'd ridden her bike across town to see him. At first, he thought it was sweet that the young kid had come to see him. Then she told him who she was. He'd told her to get out.

He'd been rude to her. He'd threatened her. But she'd stood her ground, her full lower lip trembling while she tried to fight back tears. She'd left his room but had come back an hour later with a burger and fries. She'd set the food in front of him, saying she bet the hospital food was lousy. She'd ignored the glares he'd been sending her way.

He relented and let her stay the rest of the afternoon, never dreaming she'd turn up again.

The next day she'd come with a deck of playing cards and a thermos of sweet tea she'd made for him. He'd started to rail at her, but her eyes stopped him. Her odd violet eyes watched him, and she stood there waiting for him to yell at her. But there was pain in the depths of those eyes, and he hadn't had the heart to throw her out. When he told her to shuffle, she had beamed at him, sitting carefully at the side of his bed so they could play on his lap tray. So instead of throwing her out, he drank the overly sweetened tea and played cards until he got too drowsy to see straight.

She came to see him every day over the next two weeks until he was discharged. They'd played cards, watched television, and sometimes she'd bring him a treat of some kind. She'd smothered tears the day he told her he was going home. She'd given him a homemade card she'd made for him and bid him goodbye. They didn't go to the same school, and they certainly didn't live in the same neighborhood. He'd not given her his address, half afraid she'd bike over to see him. That day in the hospital was the last time he saw little Izzy.

Little Izzy was now grown. Isabelle was an incredibly attractive woman, and she still had a soft core inside of her. He'd seen it a few times over the last couple of weeks as they'd worked together. She cared about the people she helped. And she was right; before yesterday, he hadn't seen sadness in her eyes. But he had seen her vulnerability. Whatever childhood feelings she had toward him had changed into very adult feelings, feelings she didn't seem to be able to mask.

* * *

Isabelle was gone for almost two hours before she came back to the hospital. She was extremely relieved that she hadn't received any more text messages from her brother. He was probably lying low for now, planning his next move.

The knot that had been living inside her belly gathered strength as she headed to John's room. No matter what happened, or how ugly, he deserved the truth. She tugged the duffle higher up on her shoulder, slowly opening the door to his room. She let out the breath she'd been holding when she saw he was awake. The entire time she'd been gone, she imagined him having a relapse.

"The doctor was in, and he said I can go home. I'm signed out and ready to go." John swung his legs over the side of the bed, anxious to get out of there.

Isabelle handed him the bag. His hair was damp, so he'd made use of the shower while she was gone. She'd done the same, needing to get the grime of the warehouse off her skin.

"Thanks." He unzipped the bag, pulling out a pair of pants and briefs. He stepped into the bathroom and emerged wearing them.

Isabelle's mouth went dry at the sight of his bare chest. She'd seen it bare last night as the nurse had cleaned his wounds. But in the daylight pouring through the windows, his chest had a different effect on her. Last night she'd been horrified to see the bruises marring his skin. Now, though the bruises still concerned her, she wanted to touch the light dusting of hair on his chest, her fingers itching to see if his body was as hard as it looked.

John couldn't help but grin at her look. Though it wasn't his intention, it didn't hurt his ego any. "I need help with the shirt."

Isabelle tore her gaze from his chest, seeing him holding the dark gray t-shirt she'd grabbed. If she had any sense, she would have grabbed a button-up shirt. Given the bruises still blooming on his torso, he wasn't in any shape to lift his arms over his head.

Isabelle nodded, taking the shirt from him. He sat back down on the bed, allowing her to reach his head. She had to get close to him, and the fresh scent of his skin from his shower teased her nostrils. She tugged the shirt over his head, but he still moaned a bit when he had to get his arms into the sleeves.

John was breathing heavily at the pain but still couldn't help enjoying having Isabelle this close to him, her fingers brushing against his skin as she tugged his shirt down. He'd been thinking nonstop about the kiss since she'd left. He'd taken a cold shower, hoping to cool himself off and help with some of the swelling from his bruises. Isabelle was biting her lower lip, looking at the bruises on his arms and face, and he knew what she was thinking.

Isabelle started a bit when John's hands slipped around her waist, holding her still when she would have stepped back. She realized she was standing between his legs, her body only inches from his.

"This was not your fault." John squeezed the flesh

under his hands, trying to reassure her. When she flinched, he knew he wasn't successful.

"But it is. I know what he's capable of. I was being selfish. I didn't want to leave. I didn't want to let him run me off. I thought that maybe for once I could have what I wanted."

"And what did you want?"

Isabelle had just enough sense left not to blurt out "you." "I like my job and I like the people I work with. I don't want to start all over again. I thought maybe he'd get bored or find someone else to harass."

John let her go when she pulled away from him. He didn't want to press her yet, but he wanted some answers. "Let's get out of here. We'll go back to the hotel and order room service."

Isabelle was torn. She didn't want to go back to his hotel and answer the questions she saw in his eyes. On the other hand, she didn't want to go back to her apartment either. She didn't want to admit it, but she was afraid Marcus might be there when she did. It had taken all the courage she had to go back there to shower and grab clothes. She wasn't feeling brave enough to try it again just yet. And since John did deserve the answers he was looking for, she nodded. She pulled a jacket out of the duffle bag and helped John with it as well. She took the bag and led him to where she had parked her car.

"Is this your car?" John looked at the car that had to be almost as old as she was.

Isabelle was a little embarrassed, so she kept her head down as she unlocked the passenger door. The car had seen better days. The rust along the tire wells was getting worse, and the interior was worn. But the engine was still holding up, and she couldn't justify getting a newer car. "Gable lets me borrow his car when I take clients out."

It was all she said, and John didn't press her. The car was small, and he barely fit inside. He slid the seat all the way back so his knees wouldn't hit the dash. He was relieved when the engine turned over.

Both were quiet on the drive back to the hotel. John relaxed against the seat and closed his eyes. He was startled when Isabelle woke him. He looked around and realized they were at the hotel.

"Guess I'm more tired than I thought." John let Isabelle help him out of the car. His body was so stiff that it was hard to get out of the tight space.

"You need to rest." Isabelle carried the duffle bag of his stuff up to the room. She was relieved when John stretched out on the bed. He looked pale and was sweating.

Isabelle pulled off his shoes, but he barely stirred. Smiling a bit, she watched him drop off to sleep.

Isabelle glanced around the room. She'd been in it before with Gable. She, too, was tired, but she didn't want to leave him alone. She could either stretch out on the bed with him, or she could take a nap on the couch. And though she really would love to simply lie next to him, she didn't think it was a good idea. Despite the kiss last night, he had made it clear he was not interested in a relationship with her, so the couch it was.

The light had shifted when she woke. She could see John had rolled over onto his side and was still sleeping. It was mid-afternoon, and she was hungry. He'd mentioned room service earlier, and it sounded like a good idea.

John woke at the soft sound of Isabelle's voice on the phone from across the room. She looked a bit mussed, as if she'd been sleeping. He glanced at the clock and realized he'd dozed off for a couple of hours.

"I ordered food. I hope you like what I picked. It should be up in about thirty minutes." Isabelle kept her back to him, her gaze focused on the view from the window.

"That should give you enough time to tell me about your brother and what's going on." Now that he was fully rested, he wanted some answers. He patted the unoccupied half of the bed.

Isabelle silently gathered her courage and obeyed. She sat on the edge of the bed, opposite where he was lying.

"The short story is that he's mad and wants to get even with me for helping the prosecution convict him of beating his girlfriend."

John digested that. "He just got out of jail?"

Isabelle turned to face him, tucking her legs underneath her and settling on the bed. "A little over three years ago, he severely beat his girlfriend. It wasn't the first time, but on this occasion, he violated a restraining order she'd finally gotten against him. His girlfriend begged me to testify against him as a character witness. I knew what he'd done, what he was capable of doing again. I felt it was important to help her. She'd come to me the last time he'd beaten her, and I was the one who drove her to the hospital and convinced her to press charges. So I did. Last month I got notice he was being released. He served three years of a five-year sentence. Shortly after that, I received a text message. It just said, see you soon. Then more came from different phone numbers. Then the other night, he saw you leave my apartment. I can only imagine what he thought when he realized who you were."

"No doubt he thought his sister was sleeping with an old enemy." John sat up so he could see Isabelle better.

"No doubt. He mentioned you by name in his last text Sunday night. The only thing I can figure is that you showed up at the warehouse while he was in the middle of vandalizing it. He probably followed me there a couple of times."

"Yet you didn't tell the police or Gable." John tried to temper the anger in his voice but wasn't doing such a hot job of it. He saw Isabelle flinch.

"Gable knows Marcus is out of jail. Marcus would call the office collect from prison when he was allowed to use the phone. He did it at my last job, and it got me fired. Gable told me to tell him if Marcus gave me any trouble, but I don't have proof Marcus sent those texts. And I swear I didn't see him following me. And I didn't think he'd vandalize the warehouse or attack you in the process. If anything, I thought he'd come directly after me after he got bored playing games."

John took Isabelle's hand, tugging her closer. "And you thought that was the better choice? You should have told Gable. But despite what you think, it's not your fault."

Isabelle just shook her head at that. "You said that before, but it is. I should have told Gable he was messaging me. We could have increased security at the warehouse."

"He just would have gone after the office, or your apartment, or something else. And you don't know if the warehouse was his main goal, or if he saw an opportunity and took it. He wanted to hit you where it would hurt the most, and that's your job. He probably figures Gable will fire you."

Isabelle gave a rough laugh at that. "Gable should fire me. The police were in contact with Gable last night. I've gotten text messages and voicemails from him on and off since. I haven't answered him yet, other than to let him know we're all right."

John brushed a tear from Isabelle's cheek. He didn't think she even realized she was crying. "We'll need to get your phone and talk to the police about this. I wasn't sure how much of what you said was true, but it sounds like you're right about Marcus. Given our history, it probably seemed like a golden opportunity. But there were at least three men there last night, including your brother. Would you know who was with him?"

She shook her head again. "I didn't see him much after I got married unless he was looking for money. After my divorce, I only saw him in the courtroom when I testified against him."

"Why didn't he go to your father? He bailed him out more times than I can count when Marcus was younger."

Isabelle sighed, pulling her hand out of his and tucking her arms around her waist after brushing the tears off her cheeks. "Dad died when I was nineteen. There were some financial difficulties, and Dad had become addicted to cocaine. The coroner said he overdosed. Shortly after

Dad's death, Mom had a stroke. She needed medical care, but I didn't have any money. A friend of Dad's, Nathan Masterson, asked me to marry him. He said he'd take care of my mom. I don't think he anticipated having to take care of Marcus, too. So when Marcus needed money, he came to me so I could ask Nathan."

John thought he vaguely remembered Nathan Masterson. "He was one of your father's financial backers, wasn't he?"

"Yes. He was the son of one of my dad's closest friends. Nathan was a bit older than me, but he seemed nice enough, and I was feeling desperate. My boyfriend, Danny, had broken up with me earlier that year, and it seemed like this was to be my fate."

It was John's turn to shake his head. "I take it good old Nathan didn't appreciate having Marcus in the family."

"No. Nathan and I got along fine for the most part until the last year. Marcus was constantly getting in trouble and asking for money. Nathan started spending more and more time away. Eventually, he asked for a divorce. He wanted to move in with his girlfriend. He said I wasn't worth the trouble."

"And by trouble, I assume he meant Marcus." John kept his feelings about Nathan to himself.

Isabelle just shrugged. "That and other things. But as part of our divorce settlement, he still pays for my mother's care, so I can't complain. And Nathan felt he owed it to my father to help take care of my mom. What Nathan really wanted was my parents' home and the acreage it sits on. I signed away my rights to all of Nathan's assets in exchange for him taking care of my mom's finances, and my mom leaving the house to him in her will. He lives there now with his wife and set my mom up in her own apartment with a home health worker who stays with her. The apartment is closer to her doctors."

John remembered her mother as well as he did her father. She was a cold, heartless woman. She also doted endlessly on her only son. "Is she the one feeding Marcus information about you?"

Isabelle couldn't say she was surprised by his conclusion. "Probably, though I haven't talked to her about it. She knows where I work. She knows my phone number. And she never forgave me for helping put her son in jail. She rarely speaks to me when I visit her. I get a status report from the home health worker, but that's about it."

John cursed. "She no doubt is encouraging him in his revenge, too. Has he threatened you?"

Isabelle choked a bit on her lie. "No. No threats."

John looked doubtful, and rightfully so. "You shouldn't be alone. It's only a matter of time before he decides to seek you out personally."

Isabelle kept her thoughts to herself. She planned to resign her position, pack her stuff, and get as far away as her savings would take her. Threatening her was one thing. Attacking John and vandalizing the warehouse was something else. She was a liability to Gable, and she couldn't bear to be the reason anyone else was hurt or the reason the project was delayed. What Gable was doing was too important.

Seeing John's battered face and remembering the awful

bruises on his chest was enough to break her heart. What if Marcus came back and attacked John again? She couldn't bear it. And what if he went after Gable? Gable had done so much for her, and this was how she repaid his kindness. Isabelle kept her own counsel, but she needed to get as far away from John and Gable as possible.

Isabelle's thoughts were interrupted by a loud pounding on the door. "I'm guessing that's Gable."

John nodded. "I called him this morning from the hospital. I told him to come by later this afternoon. We need to figure out what our next step is. And I asked him to pick up the new phone I ordered since I had to cancel mine."

Isabelle hadn't even thought about the stolen phone. She climbed off the bed and went to unlock the door.

Gable stormed into the room. He briefly looked at John, then turned his attention to Isabelle. "I want to know what is going on, and I want to know now. I told you to tell me if Marcus was harassing you. You ignored that very simple command, and this is what happened."

Isabelle was taken aback by Gable's tone. She'd never heard him yell at anyone. Her throat constricted and she couldn't respond.

"Do you have any idea how much damage he did? Half the contents of the warehouse are destroyed." Gable paced back and forth in front of Isabelle, then stopped in front of her again. "Well?"

John got out of bed and put himself between Isabelle and Gable. "You need to calm down."

Gable glared at John but backed off. He ran his fingers

through his hair and dropped onto the nearby sofa. "I can't believe this happened."

"Blaming Isabelle for her brother's actions won't solve our problems." John took Isabelle's hand and tugged her to the chair opposite Gable. He sat in the matching one beside her. "Everything in the warehouse was insured. I made sure of that. What we need to focus on now is how we deal with Marcus."

Isabelle spoke. "We don't have proof. All I have are a few text messages. Unless the police find that the cell phone numbers are under his name, all we have is speculation. And before Sunday, there weren't any specific threats."

John interrupted. "I checked the messages on your phone while you were sleeping at the hospital. What threats he made are vague. He mentioned me by name, but let's face it, everyone on the project knows me, so that doesn't prove anything one way or the other."

"I thought he'd come after me. I never imagined he would vandalize private property unless it was mine."

"Well, you were wrong, weren't you?" Gable got back up and paced some more.

"I think we should continue this discussion at the office. She's been through enough for one day."

Gable turned angry eyes on John, but then the fire suddenly burned out. Gable turned to Isabelle. "Are you all right?"

Isabelle just nodded. She felt exhausted, and she wasn't the one who'd been attacked.

John stood, taking command. "Get Cindy and Melissa on the phone with the insurance company. I'll get on the phone with my security company. The security at the warehouse is pathetic. Had there been a few people guarding the warehouse instead of an absent solitary guard, Marcus and his friends would never have gotten in."

"How do you think they got in?" Gable wasn't quite ready to drop the subject.

"I'd guess he bribed the security guard. There was no one there and the alarm wasn't set when I arrived. So unless the alarm wasn't set from the last time someone was there, that means someone shut it off."

"Stan's people watch the warehouse. I'll get on the phone with him and let him know he's got a personnel problem. And he'd better do something about it, or I will."

John and Isabelle watched Gable storm out of the hotel room. Isabelle wasn't surprised by Gable's anger. He was right. She should have told him. The best thing for her to do now was to get away before Marcus caused any more trouble.

"I should go back to my apartment." Isabelle went and picked up her purse.

"You shouldn't go back there alone. He could be waiting for you." John went to grab his wallet, but Isabelle stopped him.

"I'll be fine. It's daylight, and there are plenty of people around this time of day. If he were going to come after me directly, he would have done so by now. You need to rest."

John couldn't fault her logic, but he felt uncomfortable letting her go alone. Unfortunately, his head was pounding again, and his vision was still blurry. "Promise me you'll pack a bag and come right back here. The couch pulls out into a bed, so there's room for both of us in the suite."

Isabelle nodded but had no intention of coming back. She tossed her bag over her shoulder and headed out the door. Tears blurred her vision as she headed for the elevator, but she knew leaving was the right thing to do. She only hoped John would forgive her one day for lying to him. And after Gable's reaction, he wouldn't be upset by her departure.

Chapter Seven

Isabelle had been gone for over an hour when his phone rang. John had been staring blindly at the television. He wasn't ready to sleep more, but he wasn't up to working at the moment. He'd tried reading his emails, but the small text on his new phone made his head hurt. He saw it was Jack and answered.

"What's up, Jack?"

There was a bit of static on the line, but Jack's words came through. "I tagged Isabelle Masterson's bank accounts earlier in case there were any odd deposits or withdrawals. She just emptied her savings account. I'm not sure what she's up to, but that seems odd considering what happened to you last night."

John cursed into the phone. The first thing he did after Gable and Isabelle left was call Jack. He wanted security sent over to the warehouse, and he wanted someone sitting near the offices in case Marcus was feeling brave enough to go there. Jack had contacts all over the country, so it wasn't hard for him to organize a team quickly through a local company. John also knew Jack was assembling as much information on Marcus as he could find while they spoke.

"She could be withdrawing the money to pay off her brother and the men who attacked you."

John heard the words and dismissed them. "More likely she's planning to run. I need to find her."

"If she's using cash, I won't be able to trace her movements. I have a local man sitting outside her apartment right now, too. He says she hasn't been back. If she's going to run, she'll need her clothes and things to do it. I can have my man detain her."

John swung his legs over the bed, tugging on his shoes, cursing again while his head throbbed. "I'll catch a cab and head over there. If she tries to leave, have your man stop her. Otherwise, just have him keep an eye out for her. Hopefully, her apartment is her last stop."

John hung up on Jack and grabbed his jacket. His phone rang again. This time it was Gable. "What's up?"

"I just got a resignation letter from Isabelle. Is she there with you? She's not answering her phone."

John stabbed the elevator button and waited impatiently. "No, she said she was going back to her apartment to grab some clothes and things. I didn't want her there alone with Marcus on the loose, but I let her go anyway. Just now I got a call from the private investigation agency that she cleaned out her savings account. She's going to run."

Gable was quiet for a moment. "After what happened, it might be for the best."

"The best for whom? You? That's cold, Gable." John stepped into the elevator and pushed the lobby button.

Gable sighed into the phone. "I care about Isabelle; it's just that her brother set us back. He could be a threat to the other staff members, too. Look at what he did to you. Are you going after her?"

"Yes." Unwilling to listen to Gable's excuses, John hung up on him.

He caught a cab on the street and gave the driver Isabelle's address. Even if he hadn't driven her home the other night, he had her address memorized from her personnel file. When he arrived, he immediately spotted Jack's guy. The black sedan, dark sunglasses, and the intensity on the man's face gave him away. Even though he hadn't asked, John wasn't surprised Jack had someone sitting outside Isabelle's apartment only an hour after he'd called him.

John knocked on the window. "She been here yet?"

Immediately realizing who he was, the man answered. "No."

John saw a photo of Isabelle on the passenger seat, along with her license plate number and the make and model of her car. He headed to the apartment building. When he got to her door, he grabbed the knob and realized it was broken. He cautiously opened the door. The small room was in shambles. He closed the door behind him and pulled out his phone. He sent Jack a text to let him know Isabelle's apartment had been vandalized.

Even if the lock hadn't been broken, he would have immediately dismissed the idea that Isabelle had trashed her apartment in a hurry to pack. He saw profanities spray-painted on the back wall. Marcus must have seen her come and go earlier today and felt it was safe to break in. In neighborhoods like this one, people minded their own business. It would have been extremely easy for Marcus to pop the lock without anyone noticing. And even if they did notice, they probably wouldn't have cared.

John didn't want to touch anything. He'd have to call the police, but he didn't trust them to handle this. Once the police left, Jack could have a team here within the hour to go over the place.

He had just hung up with the police when he heard the door open behind him and a very feminine cry of despair.

Isabelle stood in the doorway, shocked at the damage done. It took a moment to register that John was standing on the other side of the room. She looked into his eyes, standing still and trembling in the doorway.

John quickly crossed the room and pulled her into his arms. Though he was sure she hadn't been here when the place was trashed, he could relax now that he saw she was fine. His hands stroked up and down her back, trying to calm her. The trembling in her limbs intensified, and her knees collapsed. He held her against him, leading her out of the apartment. Thankfully the hallway was empty.

Isabelle leaned against John; all fight had gone out of her. She had spent the last couple of hours cleaning out her bank account and emptying her safety deposit box. She'd even put a hold on her mail. All that was left was to pack up her clothes and grab the television she'd just bought. The dishes in the kitchen were minimal, secondhand, and not worth taking. The furniture had come with the apartment, except for the bed. Had it fit in her car, she would have dragged it out with her. But from what little she had seen and absorbed, there wouldn't be much left to pack up.

"It's going to be all right," John murmured in her ear,

hoping the words would help calm her.

Isabelle gave him a jerky shrug, and her voice was a whisper when she found it. "It doesn't matter anymore. He isn't going to stop."

John set her away from him, looking into her eyes. She seemed to get a hold of herself, the shock he had seen there earlier fading away. "The police should be here any minute. Between what happened to me at the warehouse and now this, they should agree to investigate your brother for the crimes."

"So what if he's caught? His lawyer will plead his sentence down, and he'll get out early because that's how the justice system works. Then he'll be right back, playing his sick games with me."

John placed his hands on her shoulders, stifling the urge to shake some sense into her. "So you thought if you ran, you'd be safe? That he'd just forget all about me and Gable's company? That's not how men like him operate."

Isabelle's eyes narrowed, and she found she still had some fire left in her. "How did you know I was running away? Did you follow me?"

John was relieved by the heat in her voice. He could answer that question honestly. "No, I didn't. But if you stop and think about it, it was an obvious choice on your part. The problem is, he may not stop just because you leave. He attacked me in that warehouse because he saw me with you. Even if you left, he knows we're either lovers or coworkers. He has to know I'm working with Gable. It's been in the papers. It's even posted on The Gables and The Heart's Way's websites."

The fire extinguished as quickly as it had flared. It hadn't occurred to her that Marcus might still try to hurt John again or The Gables simply because he hated John. Defeated, she sank to the floor, tucking her knees to her chin.

John squatted down in front of her. "We'll figure this out. And I have a private investigation firm looking into Marcus and his whereabouts right now. We'll get the proof we need to have him arrested."

Isabelle trembled again when John brushed the back of his fingers across her cheek. How desperately she wanted to cling to him, to believe that he could make all this go away. Whether she liked it or not, John was now involved in her problems. He was right; running wasn't going to fix this.

It didn't take long for the police to arrive, and Isabelle let John go over what happened at the warehouse, the text messages she had been receiving, and the latest vandalism to her apartment. Isabelle hated the weakness in her legs and the trembling in her limbs, but she just couldn't seem to get a hold of herself. Right now, it was all she could do to stem the tears that wanted to come.

John watched Isabelle as she watched the police process the scene. He wanted nothing more than to hold her, but he needed to focus on what needed to be done here. Isabelle was answering their questions while her eyes stayed away from the wreckage of her apartment.

Both of them were relieved when the police asked their last question and left.

John took Isabelle's hand and led her further into the

apartment. "I'll help you pack."

Isabelle stared blindly around the room. She watched John as he laid her suitcase on the bed, grabbing items from the floor that hadn't been ruined. What was the point? Almost everything had spray paint on it. Her clothes were ruined, the couch was ruined, and even the sheets on her bed. She wanted to run; she wanted to scream.

John's gentle tone interrupted her spiraling thoughts. "Go into the bathroom and pack up your things. They didn't touch that room."

Taking a deep breath, Isabelle did as she was told. It seemed so much easier to follow John's orders than it was to argue. She didn't care what he put in the bag. Nothing in the apartment held any sentimental value. She'd learned long ago not to get attached to things. But common sense told her she'd need her toothbrush, shampoo and conditioner, deodorant, and other essentials.

In short order, John packed up her suitcase. She'd probably need a trip to a clothing store to fill out her wardrobe, but this would do for now. He had doubts the spray paint would come out.

"I need your apartment key and your car key." John tucked her into his vehicle, not wanting her to drive in her current state.

"Why?" Isabelle fumbled in her purse and handed her keychain to John.

"I'm going to have someone drive your car to the hotel. I don't think it's safe to leave it in the lot at your apartment. And I'm going to have an investigator go through the apartment in case the police missed something."

She supposed John had the right of it about her car, though she wasn't sure what the point was in having an investigator go through her apartment. If the police didn't find anything, she doubted the investigator would.

Isabelle was silent for a few moments, then it dawned on her that John had been waiting for her. "Why were you at my apartment?"

John heard the demand in her voice but kept his tone soft. "I knew you were going to run, and I was hoping to stop you."

"How?"

"Gable called me and told me you resigned. It wasn't hard to figure out what you were up to after that."

Isabelle was quiet for a moment, then her temper kicked in. "So if I quit, what were you doing at my apartment? It's over. I no longer work for Gable, so you shouldn't care one way or the other what I do. You work for him, not me."

John bit back an angry retort. "Whether you work for him or not, you're not in this alone."

"Why?" Isabelle replied in a shrill cry.

"I care." John glanced over at her. It made his heart ache to see her arms wrapped protectively around herself.

John's soft, calming tone was her undoing. She pressed her palms over her face and began to cry.

John's heart broke at the sight of Isabelle weeping quietly. She hardly made a sound as the tears fell, but her shoulders hunched and occasionally jerked.

By the time they reached the hotel, Isabelle's tears had dried up. She wasn't prone to weeping. And she wasn't used to feeling sorry for herself anymore. Once upon a time, she had been great at both things, but she'd become a stronger person over the trials of the last couple of years.

Isabelle let John guide her back to his hotel room. She had her toiletry bag over her shoulder, while John carried her suitcase. When he closed the hotel room door behind them, she ignored him and went straight to the bathroom, closing the door softly behind her.

Now what, Isabelle wondered. She took a good look in the mirror. Her face was blotchy from crying and her eyes were puffy. But the worst part was she didn't know what to do. Did she stay and hope John's investigator could prove Marcus was behind the attack and vandalism? Did she take off like she had prepared herself all day to do? Would Marcus leave Gable and the organization alone? And what of John? She couldn't imagine Marcus leaving him alone after what he'd done at the warehouse. Marcus might get bored if John didn't make himself a target. But Isabelle had a feeling John would do just that if it drew Marcus out of hiding.

A brief knock on the door had her turning away from the mirror. The door opened slightly, and a man's robe dangled from John's hand.

"You should take a hot bath and try to relax." John didn't enter the room; he simply held the robe. He was happy when she took it from him. He closed the door once again.

Isabelle held the robe, unsure of what to do. She didn't want to take a bath, but a hot shower might ease some of the chill she felt. She didn't have to make a decision right this minute, and the longer she stared at the shower, the more appealing it looked.

Isabelle didn't spend a long time in the shower, but it did ease some of the chill. But instead of reviving her as she had thought, she now wanted nothing more than to crawl into bed and go to sleep. She hadn't slept much since Saturday night, and with all the tension and stress, she was feeling stretched to her limits.

She pulled the robe on, smiling a bit at how much it dwarfed her. She had no doubt the robe belonged to John. Funny, she hadn't pegged him as the type of man to wear a robe. She imagined he popped out of bed in the morning and got dressed and ready for the day. Robes were worn by people who lingered over coffee and took their time to greet the day. But the warmth of it, the lingering scent of his body on it, soothed her frazzled nerves.

Isabelle left the bathroom, a bit nervous now that she would have to face John again. She glanced around the room, but she didn't see him. She glanced over at her suitcase and saw a note on it. John had gone to fetch dinner. Grateful for the reprieve, Isabelle sat down at the nearby table and watched out the window. The traffic around the hotel was busy this evening, with people bustling past the window. The workday was over, and people were out enjoying themselves.

Isabelle started when the door opened behind her. Her mind had been drifting as she watched the people below. John held a couple of white paper bags, and whatever was in them smelled wonderful. As nervous as her stomach was, her growling stomach was letting her know it had been neglected.

Both were quiet as John laid out their meal. He'd gone to a family-style restaurant down the street and picked up a light meal. His stomach hadn't been feeling so well since he'd been kicked in the gut. And he had a hunch Isabelle's wasn't doing much better. He figured a little soup and fresh bread would do the trick.

Isabelle gave him a quiet thanks as she opened her cup of soup. The creamy potato soup looked appetizing, and she dug in. She gave John another thanks when he handed her a slice of bread. The pair quickly finished the meal.

Isabelle sat still; John's robe wrapped around her. She supposed she should have gotten dressed while John was gone, but it seemed too much of an effort to get up and dig her clothes out of her suitcase. And given that someone, probably Marcus, had his grubby hands on them, she wasn't eager to put them on.

John watched Isabelle as she kept her head down, her hands folded in her lap. She was twisting the belt of his robe between her fingers. The nervous gesture made him angry. Not at Isabelle, but at Marcus, or whoever was responsible for making her this way. Isabelle had been a sweet child, and she'd grown into a sweet adult. She worked for a charity, she kept a tidy home, and she loved helping others. And this is how she was rewarded for it. Her brother had vandalized her job, beaten John up, and wrecked her apartment.

John rose and came around the table. He took Isabelle's hand and pulled her to her feet. Carefully he lifted her chin with his fingers, lightly stroking the skin of her neck.

"Izzy." John's voice was soft in the hotel room.

John's tone had her focusing on his eyes. He was holding her so close to him, their bodies touching. She wanted to lean into him and take some of his strength. Her legs were trembling again; her strength had left her body as she'd curled up in the chair. Fatigue pressed down on her now, her body unable to take any more stress.

Before either of them realized his intention, John gathered Isabelle closer, his head bending to hers. He'd kissed her in the hospital, a rough, punishing kiss for the fear he'd felt knowing she'd entered that warehouse alone to find him. This kiss was different. At first, all he could think about was that this was little Izzy, the sweet kid who'd needed a friend all those years ago. Then he began thinking that sweet little Izzy wasn't so little anymore. She was a grown woman, an appealing woman whom he'd been fighting his attraction to since the first time he'd seen her. Somehow the fact that they were working together no longer mattered. He wanted her, and the time for fighting his attraction to her was over.

When Isabelle felt the lightness of his kiss, she wanted to cry because it felt like the kiss of a friend. But quickly the friendly kiss became something more. She still wanted to cry, but it was because the kiss was exactly what her battered emotions needed. This was the kiss of a man who desired her. Isabelle lifted her arms around his neck and held on as tightly as she could.

John backed Isabelle against the wall behind them, pressing the full length of his body against hers. She was bare under the robe, her unconfined breasts crushed against his chest. He could feel the tightness in them as her arousal grew. He hadn't meant to let the kiss get so far out of control, but control was not something he seemed to have much of at the moment. Isabelle's fingers were clenched in his hair, the tension from her hands almost painful. It was only fair because his fingers were digging into Isabelle's hips, bringing her lower body closer to his. He could hear her breathing growing faster and more ragged. His breathing was just as uneven as the pleasure built between them. He hadn't done anything other than kiss her, and he was already halfway to the point of no return.

It was a toss-up who was more annoyed by the knocking at the door, John or Isabelle. John's eyes were heated as he looked down into Isabelle's face, her lips red and swollen, the exposed skin of her neck flushed pink. John practically growled as he let her go.

"I have a feeling that's Gable." John grabbed the collar of Isabelle's robe, his robe, and adjusted the neckline. Her breasts were only slightly exposed from where the robe had parted from his hands digging into her hips, but even the hint of the upper curves of her breasts was too much of a temptation.

John went to the door and opened it. Sure enough, it was Gable on the other side of the door. He gestured for the man to come inside.

Gable's eyes went to Isabelle, who sat at the table. Her hands were holding the lapels of her robe together. Her skin was flushed, and her hair was mussed. It didn't take much imagination to realize what the two had been doing before he arrived. Gable turned to John. "I see you found her."

"Did you doubt it?" John went to the sofa and sat down.

Gable gave a slight laugh, but there was no humor in it. "Knowing what I do about you, no. I guess I am not surprised you found her."

Both men watched Isabelle as she rose. "I'm going to get dressed."

Isabelle grabbed her suitcase and disappeared into the bathroom.

"I may not be surprised that you found her, but I am surprised you're sleeping with her." Gable didn't bother to keep his voice down. Finding his project coordinator in John's robe, in John's hotel room, threw him for a loop.

"For one, I am not sleeping with Isabelle. And if I were, it would be none of your business. And just to be clear, she isn't your project coordinator anymore. You accepted her resignation. Remember?"

Gable sat. "I was upset, and maybe I spoke a little hastily. I do think it's best if she removes herself from the company until this is resolved. But there is no reason she couldn't come back when it is."

John shook his head. "You have a difficult task in front of you. Isabelle is not impulsive. And if I gauged her right, she isn't going to simply walk back into your office as if nothing happened."

Isabelle walked out of the room, hearing the tail end of their conversation. She hadn't gotten a response to her resignation, but after Gable's behavior earlier, it was a sure bet he'd accepted it. "I won't be coming back."

Her soft voice carried over the men's conversation. Gable rose. "Look, Isabelle, you have to understand the position you put me in. You're a liability."

"That's not the worst thing I've ever been called. But in this case, you're right. But the reality is that this is never going away. Even if Marcus is proven guilty of attacking John, how long do you think he'd be in prison for? A couple of years tops. And then what? I resign again? Forget it. I don't plan on hanging around once he's caught."

"But you plan to stay until he is?" Gable looked over at John, but he couldn't tell what he was thinking. Gable jerked his thumb at John. "You'll stay for him?"

Isabelle nodded. "I owe him that much for what Marcus did to him. And I owe you for what he did to the project. John said running wouldn't stop Marcus, and he's right. But for now, I can remove myself from the company, and that is what I'm doing."

"Fine. I accept your resignation." Gable turned to John. "But I won't accept yours. We have a contract."

John agreed. "Yes, we do. And The Heart's Way will see the project through. What you're doing is important. And if I can get Isabelle to agree, she'll continue to help me launch this project."

"But I quit." Isabelle wrapped her arms around her waist, holding in the pain she felt at Gable's acceptance of her resignation. It had hurt when she'd sent the email. It hurt worse now.

John faced her, ignoring Gable's frown. "You quit The Gables, yes. But I won't let you quit on me. In certain cases, I'm authorized to bring on consultants. I want you to consult on this project. You'll be on The Heart's Way payroll."

Stunned, Isabelle dropped her arms. "Why would you do that?"

"You know the people involved in this project better than anyone, even Gable. Gable has been a figurehead in his organization for quite some time. He has left a lot of the daily work to you and your team. Gable brings in the money, but you're the one who keeps the projects on task. You can do that working for me."

"I need to think about this." Isabelle dropped onto the sofa, tucking her legs underneath her.

"We'll discuss it when Gable leaves." John turned to Gable.

"I can take a hint." Gable headed for the door. "I am sorry about this, Isabelle."

Isabelle nodded but didn't say anything. She couldn't blame him. And she couldn't go back to the office after everything that happened. She might not have vandalized the warehouse, but it was her fault.

"Done thinking about it?" John locked the door behind Gable.

"I just can't, John. I can't face them." Isabelle's voice cracked as she fought back tears.

John sat and took her hands in his. "I know how you're feeling. You feel you let the team down. That you failed. But you can help fix this mess. Please?"

Isabelle was startled by John's plea. He was serious. "But how can I help if I don't work for Gable? People will find out quickly I quit. They won't want to work with me.

They probably won't trust me when they find out what happened. And they will find out."

"I'll let Gable worry about damage control. If he spins it right, he can turn this around in his favor. Donations will pour in if he plays his cards right." John wasn't worried about Gable's public relations problems. John needed to focus on finding Marcus before he caused any more trouble.

"You're supposed to be heading home this weekend. What are you planning to do?" Isabelle glanced down to see her hands still clasped gently in John's. Her fingers tightened around his.

"I've been thinking about that. I've done almost everything I can do here right now. There's no reason not to head home. I'll need to come back for the big fundraiser and gala ball in two weeks, but otherwise everything else I can do remotely."

Isabelle was surprised that he would leave with all that had happened. On the other hand, he had to be tired of living in the hotel and anxious to get home. "So how does the contractor thing work?"

"I was hoping you would ask that. First, we need to go to your apartment and clear out the rest of your stuff. Then you need to get out of your lease. That shouldn't be too hard given the circumstances. Then you need to come with me."

Go with John? "Go where?"

"My home. We'll get you settled in, and you can finish coordinating the projects you've been working on. You can work with Melissa. She'll still be at The Gables, and with you with me at The Heart's Way, you two can tag team.

Then you can come back here with me for the gala."

Surely, she'd heard him wrong. "You want me to go home with you?"

John leaned over and placed a heated kiss on her down-turned lips. "Hmm. Yes, I want you to come home with me."

She pulled away from him. She was confused by his sudden turnaround. Last week he'd kept his distance. Now he was kissing her like he had the right to and was talking about her moving in with him.

John allowed her some distance. "Just say yes. We'll work out the details later. You were going to run away anyway, so you'd have lost the apartment. You were ready to leave, so why not leave with me?"

She supposed he had the right of it. She'd been prepared to give her life up, such as it was. And she needed to be honest, at least with herself. John's offer was appealing. He was appealing. She was already in love with him. He already had the power to hurt her. She could go with him and see where the future took them. Or she could refuse and go off on her own. Of those two choices, regardless of the outcome, she'd choose John. She had no illusions that he was in love with her. They barely knew each other, though her heart didn't seem to care. The thought of never seeing him again made her heart ache.

"All right."

John was surprised by how quickly she gave in. He'd expected more of an argument, though he had intended to win it. "Good. We'll clean out your apartment tomorrow."

John glanced at the clock. "It's late. We should head to

bed."

Half an hour later, Isabelle was lying in bed alone. John had opened and made up the sofa bed right before he kissed her goodnight and turned out the lights. Isabelle wasn't sure if she should be glad or upset that he hadn't tried to pick up where they'd left off before Gable came. She'd been ready to give herself to him: heart, soul, mind, and body. Her body still hummed with residual desire. But given all that had happened, and all that was yet to come, perhaps he was right in keeping their relationship professional. As soon as the contracts were signed, she'd be his employee and he would be her boss.

Isabelle took in and let out a deep breath. She didn't think things could get more complicated than they were now. At least, she hoped not. Isabelle drifted off to sleep with thoughts of John whirling through her dreams.

Chapter Eight

Isabelle found herself back in her apartment the next morning. She knew John would be true to his word and help her clean it out. He'd picked up boxes for her so she could pack and ship anything she wanted to keep.

What did surprise her was the incredibly large, dark-haired man who was waiting for them when they arrived. John wasn't a small man by any means, but this man made John look small. He had to be at least six feet five. He looked like he worked out every day and ate proverbial nails for breakfast. This was not a man a sane person would mess with.

John entered the room but didn't seem alarmed. He looked pleased to see the other man. "I wasn't expecting you to show up."

The tall man's eyes danced with humor. "Normally you bring me boring cases. A little money laundering, or a bit of fraud. How could I resist making a personal appearance? You brought me vandalism, assault, burglary, and a damsel in distress. It doesn't get much more exciting than that. I took a flight last night."

John laughed and shook the man's hand. "No, I guess not."

Isabelle realized that the two men were good friends.

She took another step into the apartment and closed the door. She was startled when the man's shockingly blue eyes fixed on her.

"This the damsel? I'm Jack Warner. An old friend of John's."

John took her left hand, bringing her to his side. "This is Isabelle Masterson. And she's my damsel."

John's tone surprised Isabelle, but Jack didn't seem to notice John's dark tone.

Jack held his hand out to her. "That's a shame. Nice to meet you."

"It's nice to meet you."

Jack answered the question in Isabelle's eyes. "I'm a private investigator. I've been working with John for the past five years. I sent one of our men out here to check it out, but this time the case seemed to need a more personal touch. We'll find your brother."

"Any leads?" John picked up an empty box and handed it to Isabelle, but his focus was on Jack.

The man's friendly tone was gone, and he was now all business. "Not yet. He doesn't have a bank account that I can find. He doesn't have a job or a phone number. The address on his parole papers has him at a halfway house for convicts. Landlord says he hasn't seen him. He checked in with his parole officer like a good criminal, but that was the last time anyone seems to have seen him. He's not due to see him again until next month."

"He has to be getting money from somewhere, unless he had cash stashed before he went to prison." John looked over at Isabelle.

"Check my mom." Isabelle grabbed random items from the floor and tossed them in the box. "Though, I doubt you'll get much out of her. She loves Marcus and doesn't believe he beat his girlfriend. She certainly won't believe you if you tell her what he's done this time."

Jack continued. "The text messages I pulled from your phone certainly hinted at a personal relationship between you and the sender. Given that you aren't married, and that your ex is out of the country right now, the only other personal relationship you have is with Marcus. It's not much to go on as far as proof, but it's a start."

Isabelle felt her cheeks heat. She supposed Jack ran a full background check on her and knew everything there was to know about her. And if Jack knew her past, then so did John. She supposed getting divorced, being homeless, and being unemployed weren't the most embarrassing things someone could know about another person, but they made her uncomfortable.

"Do you think it's possible that any of those text messages came from your mother?" Jack asked.

Isabelle shook her head emphatically. "No, she's a lot of things, but she wouldn't threaten me like this. She's also in a wheelchair, so she didn't vandalize my apartment. Honestly, she'd tell me off to my face. She has more than once. She doesn't play games like this. Marcus is the one for games."

Jack had a tablet and was writing down what she was saying. Not wanting to focus on him, she went back to packing.

"There's not much here. Anything stolen?" Jack set the

tablet down and leaned over to help her.

Isabelle was once again startled by his intense blue eyes focused on her. He loomed over her, even though he was squatting down on the floor the way she was. "There wasn't anything valuable to steal. You investigated me, so you know I was homeless until last year. I lost everything except for my car."

"Homeless?" John strode over to her. "Your address was listed as Stan Oakley's. The man I met at the party the other night."

Isabelle blushed. "Stan let me use his address so I could find a job. You have to have an address or people won't hire you. But I never actually stayed there. Stan offered, but I refused."

John felt a bit of tension leave him. She hadn't been living with Stan. She hadn't been sleeping with a man old enough to be her father. He told himself again that it was none of his business if she had been, but he didn't believe it.

Jack looked up at John and smirked. "Okay, so the two of you are just friends. Did he know Marcus?"

"No, he never met Marcus. I met Stan while Marcus was in prison. I never mentioned him to my mom either, so she can't have told him about Stan."

"Ok. So Gable and John are the only ones who know about Marcus. And your mom is the most likely source of Marcus's information. I checked into your ex-husband's phone records and emails, but nothing from Marcus was there. They don't seem to be in touch. Miss anything so far?"

"No. I'm not a complicated person. And don't worry

about Nathan. He hates Marcus and wouldn't go out of his way to help him." Isabelle folded up the box and grabbed another.

John took the filled box and set it by the door. He glanced around. She wasn't kidding about losing everything. There were no trinkets, no mementos. The television was cheap, the furniture came with the apartment, and the kitchen only held enough dishes to feed a couple of people at one time. He never saw her in jewelry, not even cheap costume jewelry. The only nice things in the apartment were her clothes, and she probably saw those as an investment. Seeing them strewn around the room, half of them covered in paint, ticked him off. Marcus had taken what little Isabelle had and tainted it.

"So what's your plan?" Jack looked up at John while he scooped up more clothing and tossed it into the box. Isabelle wasn't folding anything, so he figured he could help.

"I need to go home for a couple of weeks. I have some other projects that need my attention. I'm going to leave Melissa here to run the show. I'm taking Isabelle with me."

"You don't waste time, do you?" Jack picked up his tablet and tucked it into his jacket. He'd seen enough. And he was a pretty good gauge of people's character. He had to be in his line of work. The way he figured it, Isabelle was exactly what she seemed. He wondered if his friend realized the lady was in love with him. Seeing John's gaze drifting back to Isabelle time and again, he figured he did. And he'd use it to his advantage to get her cooperation.

"No." John glanced around the now mostly empty apartment. "Anything else you want to take?"

Isabelle shook her head. She wanted to take the television but knew that it was silly and completely impractical. It wouldn't fit in a box and would cost a fortune to ship. She was just feeling emotional right now. She'd let the next tenant enjoy it.

The trio walked downstairs, each man carrying a box. John had gotten her out of her rental agreement, threatening lawsuits for negligence in the security of the building. The couple hundred bucks John slipped the landlord had sealed the deal. Even in this part of town, the apartment would go fast. She looked back, feeling a little sad.

John put his box in the trunk and then took the one from Jack. After slamming the trunk shut, he gathered Isabelle against him. She leaned into him, resting her cheek on his chest. Without saying a word, John knew she needed him to hold her for a moment.

"What's your next step?" John stroked Isabelle's hair while he spoke to Jack.

"I'll stay in town a couple of days and then head back. I'll visit the mother and see what she knows. When I get back, we can meet at your office. I should have a pretty good handle on how to find Marcus by then."

"Sounds good." John shook Jack's hand again, and Jack headed for his rental car.

"Let's get these boxes mailed to my address and get you a plane ticket." John eased Isabelle away from him. Her eyes were dry, but the sadness was back again. He hated seeing the light in those pretty violet eyes of hers dim.

"I hope you know what you're doing. Because I don't."

Isabelle slid into the car when John held the door open for her.

John walked around the car and got behind the wheel. He gave her a grin. "I usually do."

With that, they headed to the post office, then back to the hotel. John ordered her a plane ticket on the same flight as his in the morning. At loose ends, Isabelle decided to take a nap.

John watched from behind his laptop as Isabelle fell asleep. He promised himself they'd find Marcus, and he'd make sure nothing ever took the light out of her eyes again.

* * *

The trip to John's home was tiring, but thankfully uneventful. They'd flown into LAX around noon. Isabelle had never been to California, never been anywhere really, and the ride from the airport to John's home was a long one. They had headed north from the airport, leaving the city far behind. He didn't live in Los Angeles, but a bit north. He said the offices of the Heart's Way Foundation were not far from where he lived.

John's home wasn't massive, but it was nice. Isabelle thought he'd have the typical bachelor pad, a condo in the city, or an apartment, but this quaint house was nothing like she'd imagined. It didn't look like he'd spent much time decorating it; the walls were neutral, as was most of the furniture. But there were books on the living room table, obviously read. There were throw pillows on the couch, though a couple of them were tossed on the floor in the corner. He had a blanket on the couch, which she was sure meant he napped there now and again.

The kitchen was a nice surprise as well. He had white cabinets and dark granite counters. The appliances were stainless steel, and the fridge was huge. She opened it but wasn't surprised to find it empty. With him away so much, he probably didn't keep it full. There were a few sodas, a couple of beers, and a few condiments on the shelves. The cabinets held some pasta, some sauce, a lone box of cereal, and not a whole lot else.

John came back from putting her suitcase in the guest room to find her in the kitchen. He saw her eyeing the empty pantry. "I don't cook much."

Isabelle was surprised to see a slightly embarrassed flush high on his cheekbones. She never would have guessed he was capable of embarrassment. It made her want to cross to him and kiss him senseless. But he hadn't kissed her again since that night on the couch, and she was unsure of what he wanted from her besides helping him with The Gables project.

"Do you know how?" Isabelle shut the pantry door and the other cabinet that she'd opened.

"Some. It just doesn't seem worth the effort when I get home from work. I eat a lot of sandwiches and quick meals. I'll show you the rest of the house."

The house had four bedrooms, with a full basement. Her bedroom was a small one at the back of the house. The other room was an office, and there was another guest room next to it. There was a large living room, a small dining room, and an eat-in kitchen. There was a guest bath and a master bath. The finished basement was unfurnished, which didn't surprise her since he lived alone. Even the washer and dryer were on the main floor, so the space went unused.

"It's a really nice house." She was completely sincere. It was a home where a couple could raise a family. Even the yard was a nice size and fenced in.

"Thanks. When I saw it, I liked it. It needed some fixing up, but I liked the location and the yard. I had the kitchen professionally redone, and the bathrooms updated. A new coat of paint on everything else, and it was good to go. The hardwood floors were original to the house and in good shape."

John cleared his throat when Isabelle stood in the middle of the living room, staring out the window. "We should go get some groceries. And when we get back, we can start running your clothes through the wash."

Isabelle nodded. She hadn't realized John was planning on her staying in his home until they'd arrived. She thought he'd take her to a hotel or something. She should have realized his intentions. And honestly, she didn't want to spend her money on a hotel room. It would drain her savings fast. She knew John was working on the paperwork to set her up on The Heart's Way payroll as a contractor, but it would be a couple of weeks before she got a check.

And if she were being honest, she wanted to stay here. She wanted to be near John. And if she were feeling like being completely honest with herself, she wanted to sleep in John's bed, not the guest room.

But that didn't seem to be what John wanted, and it was

probably a bad idea now that he was her boss. Instead of saying all the things she was thinking, she nodded her head. "Groceries are a good idea. So is the laundry."

Isabelle followed John to his car, wondering how in the world she had ended up living with John Bannon fifteen years after they'd met. She smiled slightly to herself and relaxed against the comfortable seat of John's car. She couldn't help but wonder where they'd both be fifteen years from now. And she couldn't help but hope that maybe they would be together.

* * *

Isabelle sat at her new desk; a shiny new laptop was open in front of her. She was having a hard time concentrating on the contracts in front of her. People were staring at her, and it was disconcerting. She wasn't sure why it hadn't occurred to her that the gossip mill wouldn't be any different here than in the other places she had worked, but it hadn't.

Isabelle blushed a bit and kept her head down. Everyone in the office knew she was living with John. She'd only been in the office for three days, but somehow it was common knowledge. It never occurred to her that people would take notice that she and John arrived and left at the same time every day. Right now it was just a rumor they were living together, but because it was fact, she was sure her guilty behavior confirmed their guesses.

People also knew about the vandalized warehouse, though no one seemed to know about John's attack. She supposed the insurance paperwork had made its way here. Emmett Trevor was not a quiet man, and even she could hear him from inside his office when the door was closed from across the office. John and Emmett had had many meetings over the last three days, so pretty much everyone in the office was aware of the investigation that was going on into the destruction. So far, her brother's name hadn't been mentioned, so she could only be grateful. It had been her experience that people didn't want to associate with family members of criminals. Guilt by association was a very real thing.

"All settled in?"

Isabelle's head jerked up at the voice low in her ear. She glanced up to see Jack smiling at her. His smile was flirtatious but seemed harmless. She couldn't help a little flutter in her stomach at the male appreciation in his eyes. "Getting there. Except for the décor, this place isn't any different from The Gables. Are you here to see John?"

Jack leaned against the wall, his ankles crossed. "He likes updates in person."

Isabelle's gaze followed Jack's. His gaze was on a pretty redhead across the room. She was sure her name was Chloe. "Friend of yours?"

"Mmm?" Jack dragged his attention back to Isabelle. "No. I've worked with her a couple of times. She's the money lady. Makes sure I get paid. Super smart. I'm not her type."

Isabelle was intrigued. This big man seemed surprisingly unsure of himself. "What's her type?"

"Someone about six inches shorter than I am who

weighs fifty pounds less, with a fancy degree from a fancy school. She's engaged to a banker." Jack shrugged. "Oh, well. What about you? Want to tick off John and have dinner with me?"

There was a definite twinkle in his eyes as he watched John approach them. Isabelle just shook her head. "I think I'm going to have to pass."

"Pass on what?" John took in Jack's grin. "Don't tell me you're hitting on Isabelle?"

"It was worth a shot. A guy gets lonely, and she sure is pretty." He shot Isabelle a wink.

"She's got better taste than that." John shot back.

"I'd have to disagree." Jack kicked away from the wall. "We do need to find a private room to talk."

Isabelle's stomach clenched. Once again, Jack switched from playful to serious in one moment to the next.

John stepped back so Isabelle could rise from her seat. He led them both to his office, closing the door behind them. "What did you find?"

"Not a whole lot, though that is what I was expecting. We did find some partial prints the cops missed. Not enough to get a positive match that would hold up in court, but enough that we can say it's a real possibility Marcus was in Isabelle's apartment that day. Unfortunately, no other evidence was recovered from the warehouse or the apartment. We did get a couple of hits on Marcus's financials. He cashed a large check recently."

"From my mother?" Isabelle was sure she knew the answer.

Jack dropped down into a chair. "Yeah. For a woman

who is supposed to be financially strapped, she found enough money in her accounts to set Marcus up. He's in an apartment on the north side of the city. Pretty nice for a guy who just got out of jail. Do you know where your mother gets her income from?"

"My ex-husband. We made a deal. As part of the divorce, he sees to her needs. I relinquished my rights to his assets in return. I also relinquished my rights to the family home. That's really what Nathan wanted. He lives in my parents' house. So long as he pays her way, he gets the house in her will."

John frowned. "Your parents lived in a million-dollar house. And that was fifteen years ago. Property values in that area went through the roof when that resort went in. She could have cashed out."

"I suppose, but she likes having Nathan under her thumb. And she likes him. They always got along when my father was still alive. Nathan likes feeling important, and having my father's house makes him feel like he is. My mom didn't care about the divorce once she knew Nathan would still be around."

"Anything romantic between them?" Jack pulled out his tablet and made notes.

That made her pause for a moment. "I don't think so. I'm pretty sure my mom was having an affair with his father, though. That was before my dad died. Not that my father would have cared. He'd been cheating on my mom for ages. Their marriage was in name only for as long as I can remember."

"That might explain the bond, then. I have to ask. How

did your dad die?"

Isabelle dropped her gaze. "Is that important?"

Jack took Isabelle's hand. His eyes were sympathetic. "I like to have all the facts. Especially when drugs are involved."

Isabelle's glance darted over at John, then back to Jack. Her voice was soft. "If you already know, why are you asking?"

"I need to hear it from you. Do you want John to leave?" Jack didn't even glance in John's direction.

Isabelle couldn't help her eyes drifting to John. "No. You'll tell him anyway, and I suppose it's best to get it all out at once. My dad started having financial troubles when Marcus was convicted of beating John. A lot of his old business partners and clients dropped him. Dad tried to keep Marcus's conviction out of the press, but we lived in a small town and that was impossible. Things just kept getting worse the year Marcus was locked up in juvenile detention. My mom blamed my dad for not keeping him out of jail. Then she blamed him for not letting her spend money the way she used to. They were fighting more often, and Dad kept threatening to leave."

"But he didn't leave. What did he do?" Jack kept Isabelle's hand in his.

"He started doing drugs. Cocaine. He was selling off stocks he owned and sold some of his cars. After that, I'm not sure where he was getting the money. Then Marcus got out of jail and things just got worse. Over the next few years, Dad and Marcus drove the business into bankruptcy. Then one night, Dad overdosed and died."

"And that's when you married Nathan?" Jack let go of her hand and started making notes on his pad.

"Yes. Marcus took off and left Mom and me to deal with the problems. Mom liquidated the business. But then she had a stroke. So I married Nathan, and he rented out the house to earn extra money. We moved my mom into a nursing facility for a while, then into an apartment with a home health worker. Nathan worked for his dad, and he did well financially. Marcus started coming around again after my marriage. He started hitting me up for money. But Nathan kept a tight rein on the money. Marcus started going to Nathan. Nathan paid him off. It seemed easier that way. Neither of us wanted him around, and Marcus threatened to hurt Nathan and his father's business. And given that Marcus was always in trouble for one thing or another, it wasn't an idle threat. But then Nathan convinced my mom to change her will so that he would inherit her house when she dies. He also got her to make him her power of attorney. Nathan controls my mom's assets and legal affairs. Then Marcus really got out of control. He ended up beating his girlfriend, and I testified against him. My divorce took place shortly after. Nathan had gotten what he wanted out of our marriage, so he felt he didn't have to put up with Marcus anymore."

John interrupted. "Does your mom know that Nathan cut Marcus off?"

Isabelle shrugged at that. "She does. But like I said, she adores Nathan. She blames me for turning Nathan against Marcus. I imagine she gets money from Nathan and then turns it over to Marcus without his knowledge."

Jack had one more question. "Does your brother do drugs?"

Isabelle raised her eyes to Jack's. "Where do you think my father got the habit from?"

Chapter Nine

Isabelle curled up on John's sofa, emotionally wrung out from telling Jack her tale. Jack hadn't asked any more questions, but she was sure he had more of them. John had given him a stern look, and Jack had dropped the questions. She had no doubt he knew the answers, anyway. John had taken her to lunch, but she hadn't been hungry. They'd finished the workday, but John had taken them home a little earlier than usual.

Isabelle leaned against the armrest and closed her eyes. She could hear John in the kitchen. He'd settled her on the sofa when they'd gotten home. He'd even pulled off her shoes and tossed a throw blanket over her lap. She hadn't moved except to get more comfortable.

John came into the living room. He knew she wasn't sleeping, but he was hesitant to disturb her.

"You may as well ask what it is you want to know." Isabelle opened her eyes to see John looking down at her.

"I'm sorry you had to go through that today, Izzy. But it's best to get the story from the source. It must have been hard when your dad died." John sat down beside her.

Isabelle tucked her legs further under her to make room for him. "It was a relief. At least at first. You knew him. He was a difficult man, more so when he was at home and didn't have to put on a show for the company's employees. You know better than most his true nature. You and your dad."

Isabelle smiled when John looked surprised. "Yeah, I know about him firing your dad and then you. The investigation into your father's allegations went on for months. But money talked, and he got away with it. He gloated about it when it was all over. I think your father pressing charges against Marcus was the only time anyone in my family had to pay for their crimes. Dad didn't take it well."

"How do you mean?" John wasn't sure where she was going with the tale.

"Marcus comes by his personality naturally. He and my dad were two peas in a pod. The thing is, they were just like my grandpa. He's the one who built the company. He made a fortune on shoddy work and high prices. He knew who to make friends with and who to get under his thumb. Had a few politicians in his pocket, too. He died when I was twelve. He passed the business and the house to his only child. Up until then, grandpa had still been running the show. Had he been alive when Marcus attacked you, he'd have gotten off."

John sat silently and listened. He simply nodded at Isabelle, who then took a deep breath.

"Marcus grew up listening to Grandpa tell stories of the 'good old days,' which were mostly the early days when he was amassing his fortune. Unfortunately for my dad, he didn't inherit Dad's common sense and business skills. Neither did Marcus. Marcus did inherit Grandpa's violent streak, which he didn't hesitate to use when things weren't going his way. Dad did the same. And you know how Marcus ended up."

"Did they hit you?" John rose, his fingers clenched.

"I was just an inconvenience. Grandpa ignored me, and Dad pretty much did the same. Marcus mostly ignored me, too."

John paced in front of the coffee table, then faced her. "You didn't answer my question."

Isabelle wrapped her arms around her waist. "Dad didn't get physical all that much with me, though there were rare occasions. Mostly he vented his anger on my brother. He told him how he was going to take over the company one day and needed to learn how to be a man. Marcus bullied me a bit but was never overly violent. Growing up the way we did, I don't suppose Marcus had much of a chance."

John scoffed at that. "We make our own decisions. Your brother liked being violent. There is never an excuse for hitting a woman."

Isabelle's voice was soft. "No, there isn't. But that's just the way it was in my house. I was away at college when Dad died, but it was a relief. Just knowing he wasn't around anymore made me feel safer."

The kitchen timer dinged, and John glanced at the kitchen doorway. "Dinner's done. You should try to eat. You barely touched your lunch."

Isabelle let John pull her up from the couch and guide her to the kitchen. Despite the seriousness of the day, she couldn't help but be impressed by John in the kitchen. He pulled something out of the oven that smelled wonderful.

"It's just a casserole." John smiled at Isabelle; he knew she was impressed he knew his way around the large kitchen. He'd taken to cooking their meals since she arrived. She claimed to not have much skill in the cooking department, and since he would have made dinner anyway, it was no big deal for him to fix their meals, though he admitted to himself that dinner was fancier with her in his home.

"For someone who said he usually eats sandwiches, it smells great."

John fixed her a plate and set it in front of her. She picked up the fork he'd placed there before coming into the living room, but she didn't scoop up a bite. He set a second plate where he would sit but hesitated to take a seat. Cursing a bit under his breath, he pulled Isabelle to her feet.

Isabelle was startled when John's arms came around her, pulling her into his embrace. She looked up into his eyes, expecting to see comfort in his gaze. Instead, she saw desire there. He hadn't touched her since that afternoon in the hotel room.

"Izzy, you're one of the strongest people I know. You lived through hell and came out stronger for it."

Isabelle tried to shake her head, but John's hands came up to cup her face. "I'm not. When my dad died, I married Nathan so I wouldn't have to face the reality of my mom being sick and the company being bankrupt. I was a coward."

"I disagree. You married a man to take care of your mom because you couldn't do it yourself. But you went into it intending to be a good wife, didn't you?"

"I suppose. I thought I could be a good wife to him and that we could rebuild my family."

"A family who didn't appreciate you or what you did. Yet you did what you had to do to take care of them. Then when your husband left, you made provisions for your mom. You got a job. You took care of yourself. Some people would have given up or abandoned those who relied on them."

Isabelle grasped John's wrists. "Don't make me into some kind of martyr, or a hero, or something. I ended up homeless."

"Because you stood up for your brother's girlfriend and made sure your brother was punished for what he did. You could have turned a blind eye." John's fingers caressed her cheek.

"I don't want to talk about it anymore. It's done. Now we just have to find Marcus and get him permanently out of your life."

"And yours." John released her face and took her hands in his. "We should eat."

Isabelle nodded and took a seat. She ate half of what he gave her, but he seemed satisfied with that. After dinner, they retired to the living room again. John usually worked after dinner. He'd given Isabelle his e-reader, and she'd spent most of their evenings reading a book. Surprisingly, their tastes were similar, and she'd found a few favorites of hers on the device.

A couple of hours later, Isabelle couldn't focus on the words anymore. She had been staring off into space most of the evening. Isabelle set the reader aside. "I'm going to go to bed."

John pushed the laptop back, and Isabelle took his outstretched hand as he got to his feet. She gazed up into his eyes when he didn't let her go.

"Izzy, can I kiss you?"

Isabelle stared up at him. She couldn't speak. The desire she'd seen in his eyes at dinner was there again. But he'd never asked her before. He'd just done it. Dumbly, she nodded.

John's lips were light against hers. Given the turmoil of the day, the kiss was meant to soothe, not arouse. Though he certainly didn't feel soothed. But this wasn't about him; it was about her. He'd wanted to kiss her every night when she'd bid him goodnight and headed to the guest room. Every night he told himself to keep his hands to himself. He didn't want her coming to him out of misplaced gratitude. But tonight, he'd told her she was strong. And she was. And despite all that had gone on in her life, she'd made a place for herself in the world and succeeded where her other family members would have failed. In that strength, he had to trust she knew what she wanted. So he'd asked her if he could kiss her instead of taking the choice away from her.

Isabelle leaned against John, letting him take some of her weight. She opened her mouth under his but didn't seem inclined to accept her invitation. She sighed when he lifted his mouth from hers.

"John, don't you want me?"

John's body ached, but he didn't want to push her. "Yes, I do. Badly. But we can't undo it if we take the next step. If we do, then we're committed. You don't strike me as a one-night stand type of woman, and I'm not a casual man, at least not where you're concerned. If we start this, there's no going back."

Isabelle trembled under his words. "What about us being business colleagues? You said you'd never have an affair with another coworker."

John smiled. "Technically we're not coworkers."

"But you are my boss." Isabelle wasn't sure why she had brought it up, but she felt it should be said.

"You're a consultant. I just happen to be in charge. An entirely different thing. Besides, I stopped thinking of you as a coworker the moment I realized you were Izzy Douglas." John flicked his thumb over her swollen lips.

"That makes less sense. I was a kid. You didn't want to sleep with me all those years ago."

"Of course not." John's thumb traced the skin above her eyebrow. "But you had spunk. And you had a soft heart. It's a heck of a combination. And you grew up into an incredibly beautiful woman, inside and out."

Isabelle closed her eyes when John's fingers traced a line down the side of her face. "So now what?"

"Now you go to bed. It's been a long day. I want you to think about us, and what a relationship would mean. I meant what I said. Before we cross that line, I want you to be sure." John took a step back and shoved his hands in his pockets.

Isabelle headed to the bedroom, confused as to what had taken place. He admitted he wanted her, but he did nothing to act on it. He said he wanted her to be sure. Well, she was the one who'd kissed him first. And, no, she hadn't thought beyond that kiss at the moment, but she had since. Perhaps John was reluctant because he was worried about the affair ending while they were still working together. But honestly, she couldn't imagine not wanting John. For six months she pined over his picture. And when he'd come into her life, everything about him appealed to her senses. And the fact that he didn't rush her into bed and understood that there would be no going back to being just friends made him even more appealing.

Isabelle lay in bed, listening for John. About fifteen minutes after she left him, she heard him head to his bedroom. She heard the shower running a few minutes later. The water turned off about ten minutes after that, and she assumed he was in bed.

Isabelle rolled onto her side, trying to ease the knot in her belly. This knot was partially nerves but mostly desire. She wanted John. She was in love with John. She'd never lusted over a man before, but John set her body on fire. And since she had the memories of the kiss in the hospital and the moments in the hotel room before Gable interrupted them, her desire for him was never far from the surface.

Isabelle threw back the covers and rose. Her nightgown wasn't sexy, but it would have to do. She couldn't lie in this bed alone anymore. It seemed John was waiting for her to make the next move, and she already knew what she wanted. She wanted John. For now and always. Always wasn't guaranteed, but now was. And now was what she was going to take.

Isabelle didn't bother knocking on his door. She

opened it enough to peek through to his bed. She knew John saw her in the doorway. He'd left a lamp burning in the living room, and the light from the hall shone on the bed. When John didn't say anything, she went in the rest of the way, shutting the door behind her. A faint light came through the curtains, so she knew he could still see her.

They both remained still for a moment. Then John flicked on the lamp beside the bed and lifted the covers beside him. Isabelle sighed in relief and went to his bed. She slipped beneath the covers. John didn't need further invitation.

Within a moment, John was lying over Isabelle, crushing her body into the mattress. The curves of her breasts pressed against him, her body arching into his. He looked down into her eyes but didn't speak. He came up onto his knees, grasping the hem of her nightgown and working it up and over her body. He tossed the garment aside, gazing down at her. He knew her breasts would be lush, and he'd felt her curves against him. He smiled at the mole on her right hip and the other one under her left breast. Her body was perfect. And now it was his.

Isabelle had realized John was nude when she'd slipped under the covers. As soon as his body had pressed hers to the bed, she had felt his unconfined erection against her thigh. Now she was gazing up at his nude body. She'd felt shy for a brief moment when he'd pulled the nightgown off, but now she was simply fascinated by his body. She knew he was fit. His belly was flat, and she could see the outlines of his muscles. His clothes fit him well, so she'd had a pretty good idea of what he'd look like naked. Her imagination hadn't quite lived up to reality. Reality was so much better. She felt nervous for a moment as he simply looked at her, but then he leaned back down, his arms drawing her up to him.

The time for soft kisses had already passed, and John devoured Isabelle's lush mouth. She met him kiss for kiss, her fingers streaking up his back before she buried them in his hair. Her taste was incredible, her body arching into his, her legs wrapping around his waist. At the rate they were going, he wasn't going to last long. He pulled her hands from his hair and anchored them to the bed. He pulled away for a moment, trying to catch his breath.

Isabelle became uncertain. "What's wrong?"

John gave her a harsh laugh. "Nothing, other than I'm about ready to go off. I need a second."

Isabelle relaxed her legs and let her feet touch the mattress. John's breathing was heavy, and he looked like he was trying to get himself under control. The sense of wonder that he was so close to the brink and all he'd done was kiss her gave her an overwhelming sense of power. She tugged her hands out from under his, stroking his chest and shoulders. He had a thick smattering of hair on his chest, and she wanted to touch. John leaned back and let her. His belly quivered under her fingers, and it amazed her once again how badly he seemed to want her.

"My turn." John bent down and kissed one of her breasts. His hand kneaded the other. Her soft sounds told him how much she liked it. He lightly bit one of her nipples, and her legs tightened around him once again.

Isabelle opened her eyes to watch John as he caressed

and loved on her breasts. Never had they been so sensitive. The tugging of his mouth and the pressure of his fingers were almost painful, but not quite. His hands ventured lower and found the moist core of her body, and all she could do was pant his name. He wasn't the only one close to the edge.

John continued to stroke her while his mouth played with her breast. Her body clenched around his finger, and he knew she was ready for him. He released her and leaned over to the bedside table. He found the box of condoms buried in the back of the drawer.

Isabelle watched as he tore open the packet. It had been a while since she'd seen a man do that. When she'd been married, she'd been on the pill. But the sight of him rolling on that condom made her body clench even more. She wanted him inside her now. In all the years she'd been married, she'd never felt like this, as if her body would explode just by having him near.

John resettled between Isabelle's thighs; her legs once again wrapped around his waist.

"Why are you waiting?" Isabelle panted the words, her body straining to bring him closer.

John didn't respond, and he didn't wait any longer. He probed the entrance of her body and slowly sank into her. She winced a bit but accepted him fully into her body.

"Did I hurt you?" John rested his forehead against Isabelle's, straining for control.

"Just a little. You're not exactly a tiny man." Isabelle's body adjusted to him inside her. Now that he was there, she wanted him to stay there forever.

Unfortunately, or fortunately, depending on how you viewed it, John couldn't remain still any longer. He pulled almost all the way out before plunging forward once again. He set a fast rhythm and Isabelle met his thrusts, her body matching his pace. Isabelle shredded his control. He wrapped one arm under her backside, his other arm anchoring his body above hers. Her eyes were closed, and her body was straining beneath him. He ground his pelvis into hers, unable to stop the incredible release that took him. Only half-aware of Isabelle's cry that echoed through the room, John brought her as close as possible and rode out the waves that had taken over both of them.

Isabelle felt John lose control just as she lost hers. She was aware of her cry of release mingling with John's harsh breaths. Her body had completely taken over, her body striving for the promise she'd sensed in John's. He hadn't let her down. Her body was humming, her insides still quivering. The knot in her belly was gone, replaced by an enormous sense of satisfaction.

It took a few moments before John could move. Isabelle was smiling at him, her violet eyes almost black in the faint light of the room. He bent and kissed her, staying where he was inside her. He wasn't ready to leave her warmth yet.

Isabelle savored the kiss, her tongue playing with his. He seemed content to stay where he was, and she was content to let him. His arm was still around her bottom when he rolled them, so she lay on top of him, keeping him nestled within her. Isabelle relaxed on top of him, the top of her head resting against his chin.

They laid that way for a while, but eventually, John separated their bodies. He got up and went to the bathroom. She took her turn and climbed back into his bed. He pulled her back on top of him, and she completely relaxed as John's fingers trailed up and down her back.

"I never imagined fifteen years ago we'd end up together like this." Isabelle placed a light kiss on his chest.

"I don't suppose either of us did. You were a kid. A cute kid, but still a kid." John stroked Isabelle's hair when she placed another kiss on his chest.

Isabelle ran her fingers through the hair on John's chest, fascinated by the springy texture. "I wasn't cute, but I'll let that go. I was short, a little overweight, and kind of a nerd."

"Yeah, but you were a cute, short, and not overweight nerd. Maybe a bit pudgy, but you outgrew it." John felt his body stirring again as Isabelle explored his chest.

"You know when I was thirteen, I wished you were my brother." Isabelle raised her head to look up at him. She was surprised when John flipped her onto her back, his body pressing hers into the mattress.

"I am incredibly happy that I am not your brother." John stroked Isabelle's cheek, his face serious.

Isabelle shifted until John was once again lying between her thighs. Her legs climbed up his until they were once more wrapped around his waist. "Me, too."

John didn't even try to resist the lure of her body. Pressed up against her as he was, he could feel her renewed arousal. He leaned over to the nightstand, pulling another condom out of the box. He hadn't thought he'd be able to work up the energy to make love to her again, at least until the morning. He was wrong. Her soft fingers stroking his chest, her naked breasts and loins pressed up against his were all it took.

Isabelle trembled a bit as he put the condom on, unable to believe how quickly she responded to his touch, the back of his hand brushing up against her intimately as he rolled the condom on with one hand. When he kissed her, his tongue tangling with hers, she trembled again. And when he probed the entrance of her body, all she could do was hold onto him. She hadn't expected him to want her again so soon, but sweat bloomed on his back, and his body was once more hard against hers.

John ground his back teeth together, trying to rein in his desire. He couldn't remember the last woman he'd been with who made him ache the way Isabelle did. And though he had already put another condom on and was practically inside her, he had to ask. "Do you want me again?"

Isabelle heard the words whispered in her ear, her face buried in his shoulder. Couldn't he tell? Her thighs were clinging to him, her arms trying to pull him closer. "Yes."

He didn't hesitate this time, sinking into her without waiting to see if he was hurting her. Her breathy "yes" was all the answer he needed. He pulled her thighs higher, surging into her as if the last time had never been. He brought her to a climax quickly, as both of them frantically tried to get as close as possible.

Completely spent, Isabelle's thighs dropped into his hands, his arms keeping her legs wrapped loosely around him. She didn't think she had the power to move. Her arms fell limply to her sides. She felt him surge into her one last time, his powerful body stiff, then shuddering on hers. When he collapsed on top of her, she didn't think either of them would be able to move. Her thigh muscles were trembling, and she was pretty sure the rest of her body was now numb.

John managed to roll off her, though it took some effort. This time she lay still at his side, her chest heaving as she tried to catch her breath.

"Okay. I'm really, really glad you're not my brother." Isabelle weakly rolled onto her side, fitting herself against John. She smiled when he kissed her forehead. She was sure he was grinning when he kissed her.

"Me, too." John felt a great lassitude come over him. He managed to sit up and pull the condom off, but that was about all he was capable of. He tossed it in the garbage can by the nightstand and settled deeper under the blanket. Isabelle's fingers still toyed with his chest, but soon the movement stopped as Isabelle fell asleep. John held her to him, enjoying Isabelle's soft breath on his skin.

John was slow to follow her to sleep, his mind focused on how best to protect her. Having her here in his house would keep her safe for a while. But eventually, they would have to go back and face her brother. But for now, John decided to let his body relax and let his mind drift off. Isabelle was safe with him, and he had no intention of letting her go.

Chapter Ten

Isabelle woke to the sound of the shower coming from the master bath. She stretched, her legs protesting the movement. She couldn't help the self-satisfied smile on her face. John hadn't been her first lover, but her previous two had not prepared her for what she experienced with John. Danny had been her first love, but they had been practically children, without the experience of a mature relationship. Her husband had only been interested in the end result. And she hadn't loved him like she had Danny. John had touched and explored her body in a way no one ever had. And if she had any doubts about her feelings for him before, they would have been banished for good. She had no doubt whatsoever that she was in love with him.

Isabelle sat up and grabbed her nightgown. She tugged it over her head and headed for the kitchen. She could smell the coffee John had set to brew last night. The pot was full, so John must have gone straight to the shower after having gotten up. She poured both of them a cup. He drank his black, but she added a bit of sugar and milk to hers.

She knocked on the bathroom door, but John didn't hear her. She opened the door. Just as she did, John flipped off the taps and slid the shower door open. She couldn't help staring at him, nor could she help the flush she felt spreading through her body. She had seen all of his body last night, but the light from the lamp hadn't been all that bright. In the broad light of day, he was magnificent.

John gave her a wicked grin and grabbed the towel. He briskly dried his hair, then tied the towel around his waist to cover his reaction to her covetous gaze.

Not knowing what else to do, she set his coffee on the counter. "I thought you might like some coffee."

"I would." But instead of reaching for the coffee, he reached for her. He took her cup and set it down next to his. He pulled her close for a kiss. His lips savored hers, his fingers caressing her shoulders.

Isabelle felt desire starting to stir in her belly, but John released her before she could decide what she wanted to do about it. The kiss had been incredibly sweet, as if he wanted nothing more than a taste. Another first for her.

"Why don't you take your turn in the shower, and I'll make breakfast." John placed another light kiss on her lips before letting her go.

She nodded at him, her throat constricting. She wasn't sure why that soft kiss made her want to cry, but it did. She watched John pull out a couple of fresh towels for her and a wash rag. Since his shower was nicer than the one across from the guest bedroom, and because the room smelled like him, she took the towels from him but waited until he left the room before she stripped off her nightgown. He might be blasé about being naked in front of her, but she wasn't ready to strip for him in the bright light of his bathroom.

They ate breakfast and made the drive to the office. Despite their lovemaking, or maybe because of it, Isabelle strove to keep their conversation light and casual. She had a feeling that if someone were to look hard enough, they would know how she had spent the night. An hour later in the office, her mind was full of images of tangled limbs and the remembered taste of John on her mouth.

"What a man wouldn't do to have a woman look like that when thinking of him." Jack was back, and he took a seat across from Isabelle, who was seated behind her desk, her gaze drifting off. It was too bad she was in love with John. This was a woman who could easily distract a man. She wasn't quite as tall as he preferred in his female companions, but her figure was lush and made a man's fingers itch to touch. But John's warning had been clear. She was his.

Isabelle blushed and tried to regain her composure. "Are you looking for John?"

"Not at the moment. I want to talk to you again. I spent all day yesterday and most of the night looking for your brother. We need to talk, but it would be better not to do it here."

Isabelle rubbed her temple. "I'm guessing I'm not going to like what you have to say. Did you track down his ex-girlfriend yet?"

Jack nodded, but instead of answering her question, he picked up her jacket and held it out for her to put on. "We'll go have coffee across the street."

Isabelle looked across the room but no longer saw John in his office. "Shouldn't we wait for John?"

Jack shook his head. "He's too close to be objective. Besides, I'd like you to myself for a little while."

Isabelle found herself smiling at Jack. He was obvious in his flirting, but she trusted him. More importantly, John trusted him. She held out her hand to him.

"That's a girl." Jack took her arm and led her out of the building. "It's not every day I get to have coffee with a beautiful woman."

Isabelle looked up at him. Once she had gotten past his size, she had realized he was a stunningly handsome man. "Something tells me if you're eating alone, it's by choice. So what happened with the redhead you were watching the other day?"

"I've always had a thing for redheads. We went out once a while back, but she's now spoken for." Jack touched the ends of her hair, not really answering her question. "Though I think I could start to like blondes."

Isabelle shook her head at him and let him guide her to a table in the corner of the small café. She let Jack take her order to the counter. When he returned with her coffee, she asked him again. "Did you find his ex-girlfriend?"

"I found the ex. She skipped town as soon as she heard he was free. I spoke to her mother. Marcus came around a few days ago but quickly vanished after that. I'm not sure how interested he is in her. I suppose had I been called onto the case sooner, I could have had her tailed. Right now, I'm focused on his financials. There is a lot of truth to the saying 'follow the money.' Other than the deposit from your mother, there hasn't been any activity on his old accounts in the past week. But yesterday that changed. I'm trying to track the new deposits. And how he came upon them. Do you know any of his other girlfriends?"

"He's always had a few in the wings, but I've never known them. He also has friends, but again, I don't know them. After my divorce, but before I testified, he stopped coming around. I didn't have anything he wanted."

Jack nodded. "This past week I've had people watching the apartment where your mother lives, but he hasn't shown. I also had a man check out his old haunts. I did find one of his latest girlfriends. He doesn't spend much time there, but as far as I can tell, that's where he's living, not in the apartment he rented."

"Does he have a job?" Isabelle thought as part of his parole, he'd have to have one.

"He did when he was released. But about two weeks ago, he stopped showing up. I made a call to his parole officer, but the man wasn't much help. He said your brother checked in with him at his scheduled time. And unless I had proof he was doing something illegal, he wasn't going to bother with him until it was time to meet again."

"He doesn't care that he's not working? Isn't that a violation?"

Jack took a sip of his coffee. "The officer said as long as he was employed when they met again, he didn't care. He's not exactly up for Employee of the Month. But I do have some good news."

Isabelle kept her eyes on her coffee. "I can't imagine what could be considered good news."

"I have ruled out your mother giving him the new money. I looked into your mother's financials, and your ex-husband pays all her bills outright. He hired a caretaker who does her shopping and runs her errands, and he gives her the cash, not your mother. Your mother has very little money of her own. Whatever money she gave him was the last of what she had saved."

Isabelle turned her head, unable to look Jack in the eyes. "As I said before, it was part of the divorce settlement. Nathan pays her bills, and he gets my father's house when my mother passes."

"And we've already established Nathan wouldn't give Marcus money. So that puts your ex and your mother in the clear."

Isabelle shrugged. "I guess that's good then. But Marcus has no job and no home of his own. I suppose his new girlfriend could be supporting him, but if she's like his other girlfriends, she's not going to have a lot of extra cash."

"You're right. The girlfriend doesn't have much money. The only money coming in is her welfare check and a little cash she makes working part-time. But I did see a large cash deposit in her account. I'm guessing it came from your brother. And yesterday he opened a new account and dumped five thousand cash into it."

"What?" That got Isabelle's attention.

"It's a pretty good chunk of money for a man fresh from prison. It's possible he stole it, but I can't help but wonder if it was to do a job."

"What kind of job would pay him that kind of money?"

Jack patted her clenched fist. "The illegal kind. I'm following that angle now. But I've found him, I know where he lives, I know who he's hanging out with, and I know he's up to no good. Now I need to find out who paid him five grand plus what he gave his girlfriend, and why."

Isabelle still wasn't following Jack's train of thought. "But what does that have to do with me or John's attack?"

Jack finished his coffee. "That would be the question of the day. And one I'm going to find the answer to. Right now, Marcus is lying low, trying to keep a low profile. He's already violated his parole, but he probably thinks John's attack, the vandalism of your apartment, and the destruction of property at the warehouse can't be proven without reasonable doubt."

"It can't. We have no proof he attacked John, or that he trashed my apartment and the warehouse."

"Ye of little faith. For starters, I took some photographs of him buying drugs. I also have proof he's been fired from his job. That will get him tossed back in jail once the proper authorities are notified. As far as his crimes against you, there were dozens of prints at the warehouse, but unfortunately, none of them were your brother's. But my man did find John's phone in Marcus's car. He helped himself to it. Your brother's prints are all over it, and so are the pictures he took of John lying beaten in the warehouse."

Isabelle gaped at Jack. Then she smiled. "So you have proof Marcus was at the warehouse because he was in possession of John's phone. But how will you prove where Marcus got the phone?"

"There's a reason investigators have licenses. My guy carefully documented Marcus in the car, Marcus holding the phone, and where the phone was obtained. It's now in police custody with a clear chain of evidence backing up its acquirement. John will identify the phone as his, and where he last had it."

"So why not just have him arrested?"

"Because it's too easy. I want to know where he got that money, and who he got it from. Before prison, he hustled for every dollar he had. He wasn't a drug dealer and isn't now. And while there are dozens of ways he could have come across that cash that have nothing to do with you, my gut says otherwise. You're safe here with John, and Marcus can't cause you harm when he doesn't even know where you are."

Isabelle wrapped her arms around her waist. "Do you think he's looking for me?"

Jack shook his head. "Not actively. It's another reason I'm wondering about the cash. If you were the reason he trashed the warehouse and beat John, you'd think he'd at least have feelers out for you. As far as I can tell, he hasn't even done a rudimentary search for you on the internet, and I have his phone tapped, and his computer tapped, along with his girlfriend's. And I have a tracker on anyone searching for you. Nothing."

It should have reassured her that her brother wasn't looking for her. Unfortunately, it just made the knot that was living in her stomach tighten more. She wanted to question Jack further, but she had a feeling he would sidestep any direct questions he didn't want to answer. She was putting her safety in his and John's hands. Knowing that she had these two men looking out for her, she felt the knot in her belly loosen.

"So, what now?" Isabelle took a sip of her coffee.

"You and John just need to keep doing what you've been doing while I do my job."

Isabelle was pretty sure she turned crimson red but hid her face behind her coffee mug. She had a feeling he knew exactly what she had been thinking when he approached her desk just half an hour earlier.

Jack smiled at her flushed cheeks. "Yeah, you should keep doing that, too. John's been alone too long. He could use a good woman in his life; keep him from working too hard. Sometimes charity work can suck you in. You see so much bad and want to do more good to counter it. But it's easy to get burnt out and forget to make your well-being a priority."

Isabelle was quiet as Jack led her back to the office. The first thing she saw was John back in his office, once again on the phone.

"Do you think you'll stay?" Jack followed her gaze.

Isabelle nodded. "Yes, I think I'll stay. And even if it's not with John, it's past time I make some drastic changes in my life."

Jack laughed. "Moving to California would be a good start. In some ways, we're a world unto ourselves."

"It's certainly different from the Midwest; that's for sure."

Jack waved at John, who just realized Jack was cozied up to his lady. "I'll let you fill John in on what we talked about. If I don't find anything concrete soon, the cops will arrest Marcus regardless. By the time you leave for the charity ball, your brother will be locked up."

Isabelle turned to him. "Thank you, Jack. I don't know what we would have done without your help."

Jack kissed her cheek and winked at her. "If you ever

dump John, look me up. I'll be in touch."

Isabelle watched Jack's retreating back. So did most of the other women in the room. He was not the type of man to go unnoticed.

"What did he want, besides you?" John came up behind Isabelle and placed his hands on her shoulders.

Isabelle turned in his arms. "He found Marcus. And he also confirmed neither my mother nor my ex-husband has been giving Marcus money, other than that first deposit."

John led Isabelle into his office. "That's good news then. We were already pretty sure about your ex, but your mother was a good candidate. What else did he say?"

"Just that Marcus is living with a woman, not in the apartment he rented, and just deposited five grand into a bank account."

"Now that is interesting. And I suppose he told you he recovered my phone."

Isabelle nodded, then slipped into John's embrace. "He said Marcus would be in jail before the charity ball, one way or another."

John kissed the top of Isabelle's head and wrapped her in his arms. "Yes. I've already identified the phone, and his prints are on it. We have your statement. And once the cops seize Marcus's phone and that of his girlfriend, we'll have proof he was texting you and threatening you."

"Did you already talk to Jack?" Isabelle pulled away only enough to look into John's eyes.

"I got his report in my email this morning. I read the highlights."

"Can I see it?" Isabelle laid her head back on John's

chest.

"Sure." John knew she needed to see the proof in black and white. No matter what, they were talking about her brother, her flesh and blood.

John led Isabelle to his seat and pulled up the files he had from Jack. "Why don't you take a look now. I have to run in and chat with Emmet about a different project I'm interested in taking on."

"All right." Isabelle waved John off when he hesitated. "I'll be fine. Go."

Isabelle waited until John left the room before she started to read the report. Jack was very detailed. The report didn't answer why he was so interested in the five thousand dollars, which puzzled her. As far as she was concerned, he fulfilled the task that had been set before him. He didn't need to keep digging into Marcus's life. But she was grateful he was. There was no doubt in her mind that he was up to no good, but Jack was going above and beyond.

All that he told her was here. The call to her mother, the investigation into her ex. There was a very detailed section on Marcus's ex and where she had gone. The woman was doing well, and that made Isabelle happy. The woman had been through so much; she could only wish her the best.

The rest of the report wasn't very informative. There were a lot of negative statements as to where Marcus was and what he was doing. There were detailed reports on some of Marcus's friends, including his new girlfriend, but nothing incriminating. Isabelle imagined that when he was arrested, he'd turn on his friends to get a lesser sentence.

He wasn't alone when he vandalized the warehouse and beat up John. She doubted he'd take full blame for it.

Isabelle closed the file. She leaned back in the chair and stared at the computer. She was about to go find John when she saw her name on a folder. The file was also from Jack. Unable to stifle her curiosity, she opened the file. Inside it were pictures of her, along with detailed reports on her past and current financial status, her marriage, her family, and her friends. There was a detailed report on Marcus and the reasons he was in prison. That wasn't surprising, given the circumstances. There were details about her mother's health and her expensive care. The report mentioned how often she visited her mother and how long the visits lasted.

In addition to that, there was a detailed report on her ex-husband. According to this, he was getting married next month, and his soon-to-be wife had borne him a child last year. She hadn't spoken to him since shortly after their divorce. So long as he kept his side of their bargain, there was no reason to contact him. But her mother hadn't mentioned a baby or an engagement. Normally her mother was very chatty about him and how well he was doing without her.

What bothered her the most was Jack's speculation of an affair between her and Stan while she had been unemployed. There was no mention of where she had been living, so it was presumed she was living with him. Jack wrote that he was pretty sure she used Stan to get her job with Gable.

Seeing the report hurt. This report wasn't about Marcus and the warehouse. This report wasn't about John's attack. This was written before either of those things had happened. John had her investigated as if she were a criminal.

Isabelle rose from his desk, closing the lid of John's laptop. Without thinking, she went back to her desk. She grabbed her coat and purse. She needed to get out of here. She couldn't face John, knowing he didn't trust her. When she got outside, she simply walked. Thirty minutes later, she found herself in a park. She took a seat on a bench and watched people go by.

She supposed she shouldn't blame John for investigating her. He didn't know her. They had met because he had a job to do. She imagined people lied to him all the time. Charlatans and people were looking to take advantage around every corner. Despite The Gables' small size, there was a lot of money coming in and out of the charity. In the time she'd worked for Gable, she'd met a lot of people trying to make themselves look good by being involved in their charity, or those who would take advantage given the opportunity.

Telling herself that wasn't a good enough excuse, she went from hurt to angry. When her phone rang and it was John, she ignored it. She stayed on the bench, taking deep breaths to get her anger under control. She expected distrust from others, but not John. She thought they had a connection, one they both had felt. Perhaps she was just fooling herself. And when her phone rang five minutes later, she ignored it again.

Isabelle closed her eyes, wrapping her arms around her waist. Not completely oblivious to the dangers of a woman alone, she tucked her purse under her coat and stayed in an open area. She knew she couldn't hide here all day, but she could hide here long enough to figure out what to do next.

"I'm going to give you one chance to tell me what in the world you think you're doing."

Isabelle's eyes popped open to see John hovering over her. His eyes were snapping fire. His voice had been low, but there was a hint of a threat in his tone.

Isabelle rose and started walking away from him. She wasn't at all surprised to find herself spun around and in John's arms. He was half-dragging, half-carrying her to where his car was parked. She could see it on the outskirts of the park.

"Leave me alone. I don't want to talk to you." Isabelle tried to free herself, but John's grip tightened on her.

"Not on your life." John opened the car door and put her in it. "Stay."

Isabelle was very tempted to disobey, but before she could decide whether she should stay or go, John was buckling his seat belt and pulling onto the busy road.

"Are you going to answer me?" John's fingers were turning white from the tight grip on the steering wheel. He forced himself to loosen his grip.

"I don't have to answer you. I don't want to talk to you."

"Why? After last night, I think I deserve an explanation."

Isabelle kept her eyes on the road as she buckled her seat belt. "I don't talk to people I can't trust."

"Trust?" John wove in and out of traffic, his anger in

no way diminishing his driving skills. This was Los Angeles after all. When Isabelle didn't answer, he dropped silent. He wanted to hash this out in private, not on the freeway.

When they pulled into John's driveway, Isabelle remained in her seat. Seeing John angry was new to her, at least angry with her. He had been plenty angry in the hospital after having been beaten up, and he'd been pretty angry when he saw her apartment had been vandalized, though both times he'd kept his temper under control. He didn't seem to have much control over it now.

"Out." John leaned over to release her belt and tugged her from the car when it looked like she was just going to sit there.

"I don't..."

John cut her off. "I don't care what you want right now. You're going to answer me."

Isabelle brushed past him into the house. She had no doubt he would have picked her up and carried her inside.

"Now what is this nonsense about trust?" John closed the door behind him and turned to face her.

"You don't trust me. You and Jack. I thought you were my friend. I thought you cared. But you lied to me."

"What makes you think that? Last night you thought otherwise."

Trust a man to throw sex in her face. And trust a man to think that he could have everything his way. "Last night I trusted you. Now I don't."

"Why?" John took two steps forward.

"I saw that report." Isabelle threw the words at him.

John looked puzzled for a second. Then it dawned on

him what she was talking about. Relief filled him. He hadn't been sure what had put her in such a twist, but he was grateful it was something as simple as that report. "Isabelle, that was nothing."

Isabelle's breath hitched as she fought tears. "It was a total invasion of privacy. And it proves you don't trust me. I'm good enough to sleep with, but not good enough to place your faith in."

"Isabelle, I run investigations on people like that all the time. Of course, I didn't trust you. I didn't know you. But that report was from before I realized who you were. Little Izzy Douglas would never do anything to hurt anyone. But I didn't know Isabelle Masterson. Trust me when I say I've dealt with a lot of shady people. I needed to be sure of you. I have similar reports on everyone I do business with."

Isabelle tried to hold onto her anger, but it was fading quickly under the sincerity in his voice. "I didn't like it."

John took the last few steps that separated them. When she didn't back away, he pulled her into his arms. "You scared me to death when you disappeared today."

Isabelle sniffed back her tears. "How did you know where to find me?" Then her anger flared again, and she struggled in his arms. "Are you having me followed?"

John soothed her. "No, Isabelle, I'm not having you followed. When you didn't answer your phone, I had Jack trace it. The phone was on, so he could track it."

Isabelle remembered the part that had ticked her off the most. "The file didn't get it right, you know. I wasn't having an affair with Stan."

"I know. I knew that for certain last night. But it

would have been okay if you had."

Isabelle pulled away. "How did you know last night?"

John kissed her lightly. "Some things a man just knows."

Isabelle wasn't sure she liked that answer but supposed that as long as he got to the right conclusion, she could live with it. She wrapped her arms around his neck and let him kiss her again.

What started as a soft kiss quickly escalated into something much more. Isabelle stood on her toes, trying to bring herself as close to John as she could. She could feel the hard planes of his body against her softer ones. Within moments, she desperately wanted him.

John deepened the kiss, lifting her so that her legs were wrapped around his waist. He continued kissing her, his hands quickly peeling her blouse and bra off her as he carried her toward the bedroom. Her hands were as avid as his, though she struggled to keep herself upright and remove his shirt at the same time while he carried her to the bedroom. He tossed her down on the bed, quickly finishing the job she'd started.

"John." Isabelle panted his name when he was finally naked before her. Her hands tangled with his as he worked to remove her slacks and underwear.

John groaned when Isabelle sat up and wrapped her hands around his erection. He stilled her exploring hands. He was already on the brink. When Isabelle tugged him down to her, he didn't hesitate to follow. He quickly grabbed a condom that was lying on top of the nightstand from the night before and quickly donned it. As soon as it was on, he plunged inside her. She lifted herself into his thrusts, both of them frantic. He could feel her nails digging into his back, as well as the sweat that was gathering there. Her body was as slick as his, her voice panting out his name. All he could think of was that it had never been like this before. He'd never had a sudden urge to mate. And that was exactly what this was. This wasn't sex. This was something much deeper.

John's hips locked against hers as they both reached the peak. At first, he couldn't speak, and neither could she. He collapsed on top of her, both of their chests heaving as they tried to get their breath back. John found his voice first. He rose on his elbows and looked down into Isabelle's face. He brushed a few loose strands from her cheek. "I love you, Isabelle."

Isabelle's mouth opened, but no words came out. Those were the last words she had expected to hear from John. She felt her throat constrict and tears form in her eyes. No one had told her they loved her since Danny. And that seemed so very long ago, almost as if he had said those words to a different woman. And in some ways, she had been a different person then. She had been just a girl. Now she was a woman. And to hear those words, especially from John, left her speechless.

Not offended or upset at her silence, John leaned down and kissed her. He wanted to go on kissing her forever. He touched her body, his hands finding her breasts, then her belly, then her thighs. He doubted he could make love to her again anytime soon, but he wanted to imprint himself on her. He felt her body tense, then relax in the places he touched. Finally, he released her mouth and rolled off her.

Isabelle stared at the ceiling. Then realizing she wasn't where she wanted to be, she rolled to her side so that she could lay her head on John's chest. They had lain like this last night, and it felt like the most natural thing in the world.

Chapter Eleven

"Do you love me, Isabelle?" John asked the question twenty minutes later, in the darkening bedroom, afraid of her answer.

Isabelle, who had been half dozing, came fully awake. She realized she hadn't responded to him. She propped herself up, resting her elbows on his chest. "I think I've loved you in different ways since I was thirteen. When I was thirteen, I loved you like I would a brother. Then when I thought of you when I was older, the feelings were hazy but pleasant. Then I saw your picture in a magazine when I was researching The Heart's Way Foundation. All those feelings came pouring back, but this time they were the feelings of a woman. Then I met you again, and all I could think about was you. Gable said I was making googly eyes."

John chuckled at that. "I noticed. I wanted to respond to those googly eyes, but I didn't think it was a good idea. I've since changed my mind."

Isabelle laid her head back down. "Good. And I didn't have to work that hard."

"I've never been good at self-deprivation. And I wanted you. One way or another, I would have had you, regardless of what I thought was best."

"That is one of the things I love about you. You go after

what you want. But what you want are good things, things that help others, not yourself. You're the least selfish man I've ever known."

John thought about that. Her father was a selfish bastard. Her brother was as bad, just in a different way. Her mother was self-centered, and her husband married her for all the wrong reasons. It was a miracle she trusted him, much less loved him. But perhaps she loved him because she could trust him. She could trust him with her love. And he supposed her knowing him when he was a surly teenager helped. He'd been mean to her, but she'd stayed. He'd eventually relented. He'd missed her after he went home from the hospital. And even though he had told himself he didn't like her, he had enjoyed their moments together. And lying on the floor, beaten and bloodied, something opened in his heart the moment he realized Izzy Douglas was looking down at him.

"So what do we do now? I can hear the gears in your brain working." Isabelle yawned and snuggled closer.

John placed a hand on her hair, stroking it away from her face. "After work this week, we'll get you a dress."

"Why?" Isabelle completely relaxed against him.

"We have a charity ball to go to for The Gables. I have to be there since I'm head of the project. And I think you should be there, if for no other reason than to prove you can't be beaten."

That made Isabelle tense, and she rolled onto her back. "Jack said he expected Marcus to be behind bars by the time we leave. The ball is in less than two weeks. I imagine we'll have to fly out a few days beforehand to get settled in and handle any last-minute details."

John picked up Isabelle's hand. "Nope. Melissa is handling everything there on our end. I had Melissa book us a room at the hotel where the ball is being held. We'll fly in Saturday morning, get ready for the ball, make our appearance, then fly back out the next morning."

Isabelle sat up, holding the sheet to her breast. "Then what? I quit my job at The Gables. I know you said I would have a job here as a contractor so long as the hospital project was underway. And not to jump the gun, but then what? And I can't just move in here indefinitely."

John pulled Isabelle back onto the bed, shifting until he was lying over her. "Do you know what love means? Love means we make a commitment. As far as I'm concerned, you're not going anywhere. And I don't want you here indefinitely. I want you here permanently."

Isabelle couldn't stop the tears that gathered and fell. "It's hard to say no when I want something so badly. But we don't know each other well. This affair is new. You may not feel the same way once the novelty has worn off."

Instead of arguing with her, John kissed her. He felt her sigh against his lips. He poured all that he felt into the kiss. Then he kissed the tears from her cheeks. "Our affair might be new, Isabelle, but our relationship is not. Even all those years ago, I felt a connection to you. And I missed you after I was released from the hospital. But I'd already signed up for the military, so seeing you again was pointless. And honestly, I don't know what I was feeling then. You were thirteen, just a kid. I was almost a man, getting ready to go into the world. But I swear to you, since the moment I realized who you were, it has felt like fate intervened and brought you back to me."

Isabelle hugged John, pressing her face into his shoulder. "I want to stay here permanently, too. And I feel like you do, that somehow, we're destined to be together. I can't explain it any better."

John rolled onto his back, pulling Isabelle with him. "You don't need to explain it. You just need to accept it. And don't worry about the contractor's job. There's always room at the foundation for someone with your skill set. And if you don't want to work for the foundation, there are any number of other jobs."

Isabelle kissed his shoulder. "I would love a job at the foundation. Working at The Gables opened up a whole new world to me, one where you could get paid and still make a difference in people's lives."

"Then it's settled. You'll move in, you'll work at The Heart's Way with me, and we'll get married." John smiled in the darkened room when Isabelle tensed up next to him again.

"Did you say married?" Isabelle lifted her head so she could look into his eyes.

"Yes, I said married. Jack can be the best man. I know you don't know many people here, but you'll make friends fast. And if you're agreeable, I have a sister who could be your bridesmaid. You're going to love my family. My mom and sister will insist on flying out to help plan it."

Isabelle had forgotten he had a sister. And if she remembered correctly, he had another brother, too. She already knew his parents were alive and well. "You're serious."

"Now that I've got my Izzy back, I'm never letting her go."

Isabelle saw the seriousness in his gaze. And she saw the question he hadn't asked her there, too. "But marriage? Isn't it a bit soon?"

"No. I don't think it's too soon. I think it's perfect. I know everything I need to know about you, and I love everything about you. I've never been an indecisive person, and neither are you. And I think we're both old enough to know what we want."

"We are also both old enough to know we shouldn't rush into anything so permanent. I'm already living here, and I'll stay. I just think we should be sure before we get married."

"I'm sure." John kissed her deeply. "And I'll do whatever it is I need to do to convince you to say yes."

Isabelle wasn't quite ready to say yes to marriage. She'd been married before, and it wasn't something you took lightly. Her heart was telling her to just say yes and give in to John. Her head was telling her to take her time, to be sure.

John kissed her again, an ache in his chest because she wasn't ready to give him the answer he wanted. "We should get some rest. As I said, we've got to get you a dress, and we have a lot of work to do in a few short days."

Isabelle saw the slight pain in his eyes. But she just wasn't ready. Instead, she ran her hand down his chest, then down his thigh. "I'm not feeling tired anymore."

John pulled Isabelle on top of him. This time

afterward, she fell into an exhausted slumber.

* * *

It was three more days before word came back on Marcus's arrest. Jack tapped the screen on his tablet and brought up the police report. "Marcus was arrested late last night by the local authorities. His bank records show a new deposit, this time three thousand in cash. He's playing coy right now with the police, trying to strike a deal."

John took the tablet so he could read the report himself. "Strike a deal for what? He harassed Isabelle, jumped me, vandalized a warehouse, and vandalized Isabelle's apartment. What could he possibly have to bargain with? Not to mention, he's on parole."

Jack looked at Isabelle, then back to John before he spoke. "He says someone paid him to break into the warehouse. He said if the cops make him a deal, he'll give up the name."

Isabelle couldn't believe what she was hearing. "But he attacked John. He broke into my apartment. Just the attack alone should be enough to negate anything he might try to bargain with."

Jack patted Isabelle's hand. "Good news is that there was blood other than John's in the warehouse. Marcus has a wound on his hand that is partially healed. It looks like glass might have sliced him up. We have glass with blood on it from the warehouse. When the DNA results come back, the police have no doubt they'll find it belongs to Marcus. But he's not stupid. And I'm guessing he learned a lot in prison. DNA tests take time, so Marcus has time to stall. He said it's big, what he knows. And he's waiting for the District Attorney to decide if they want to make a deal or not."

"Did they find his phones? The ones he used to harass Isabelle?" John pulled Isabelle to his side. She was trembling.

Jack nodded. "They did. Harassment charges aren't much, but the cops charged him anyway, just to pad the list of crimes. And they have your phone and my chain of evidence as proof he stole John's. And since he was so kind to document the attack, the police have photographic evidence linking the crime scene on the phone of the attack back to Marcus. There's nothing tangible to link him to Isabelle's vandalized apartment, but no jury is going to believe he wasn't behind it."

Isabelle leaned against John, taking comfort from his presence. "What do they think Marcus has to bargain with?"

"Who would benefit from the warehouse being vandalized? Who might have paid him and his cronies to do so?" Jack took his tablet back from John.

John thought about it. "Stan Oakley, the owner, might if he was trying to get out of the contract he'd signed. He was renting that warehouse dirt cheap. If he had a better offer, he might try to force the tenant out. Or it could be someone opposed to the hospital. Not everyone is going to be happy that a new, very large structure is going to be built so close to other valuable real estate, especially when other real estate would be more profitable."

Jack agreed. "Those two options are very likely."

Isabelle heard something in his tone. "But that's not what you think."

"No, that's not what I think. And it's not what John thinks, either. But I'd rather not say what I think until I'm sure."

John shook his head at that. "I think it's better to get it all out now. The only other person who could benefit from this is Gable Lockwood. And because it was Marcus who was paid to vandalize the warehouse and not a random thug, we can tie Marcus to Gable through you. It's a bit of a stretch to believe a stranger would hire Marcus to vandalize the warehouse without knowing how he is tied to you."

Isabelle's head jerked up. "Gable? There's no way he would do this. He wants this hospital built more than anyone. Why would he pay my brother to vandalize the warehouse?"

Jack agreed it was best to get it all out now. "I'm sorry, Isabelle, but it's the only scenario that plays. And if the D.A. makes that deal, we'll have corroboration from your brother that it was him. I expect the offer to come down later today. He'll still go back to jail, but he'll plead down to a lesser sentence and not do as much time."

"I don't understand. Why would Gable pay my brother to beat up John?" Isabelle turned heated eyes to Jack.

"I don't think he did. I think Marcus saw a golden opportunity. John was just in the wrong place at the wrong time. It was simply too good an opportunity for Marcus to pass up. He got paid to vandalize the warehouse and got revenge on an old enemy at the same time, one he's convinced is sleeping with his sister."

"A sister who betrayed him by testifying against him." John wished he could spare Isabelle this.

Jack tried to temper his voice when he spoke to Isabelle. "Exactly. Gable knew your brother was getting out of jail. And let's face it, Gable isn't the type of man who would know how to go about hiring a criminal. He would have seen something wasn't right with you. He would have known what that something was. He probably swiped your phone and used it to contact your brother. He made him a deal he couldn't refuse. And it wasn't as if anyone was going to tie Gable to Marcus."

"But you did." Isabelle felt angry, but mostly she felt confused.

Jack did his best to convince her. "Look, Marcus got out of jail and harassed you. I doubt it would have gone beyond that. Marcus is on parole. I don't think he would have come out in the open and hurt you, risking going back to prison. But when Gable approached him with a cash offer, everything snowballed from there. He vandalized the warehouse. He jumped John when the opportunity arose, then decided he'd already caused enough trouble, so why not vandalize your apartment, too, just for good measure."

Isabelle pressed her face into John's chest. There was so much pressure in her chest that she couldn't breathe.

John stroked his hands over her back, trying to soothe her. "I know it's a lot to take in, Izzy, but it's the only thing that makes sense. Jack ran Gable's finances. At first, nothing stood out. All his accounts seemed in order. But then Jack dug deeper and found offshore accounts and other hidden assets that are all being used as collateral against several loans. And what has value that wasn't being used as collateral, Gable has since sold. He's even cut back on his personal expenses. On a hunch, Jack dug into the foundation's finances and found that Gable siphoned money from the foundation to cover his debts. Medical care is not cheap, and he knows that better than anyone. His daughter's bills have been excessive over the years. He overextended himself, and he used the foundation to cover that debt. Now he has to pay it back. Large projects like hospitals will involve large budgets and regular audits. I don't know if he realized that by involving The Heart's Way Foundation, we'd be looking into his money situation as closely as we did."

Jack finished for John. "And an insurance payout was the quickest way to get money back into the accounts. With some creative accounting, the missing money could have been shuffled around a bit and then covered by the insurance check. Then he could use the vandalized warehouse to get some free publicity. He could garner sympathy from the community, and in short order, he could have not only had his finances back on track, but The Gables' hospital project would still be underway, with minimal delays."

Isabelle rubbed the tears from her eyes. "So you need Marcus to corroborate your theory. And to do that, the state will cut him a deal."

John pushed the hair back from her face. "Yes. Jack is good at what he does. The police have enough evidence against Marcus to tie him to the warehouse. I'm pressing charges for assault, so he has that to contend with, too. He'll give up Gable. And by the end of the day, Jack will have proof that Gable took out the exact amount of money from his accounts that Marcus deposited."

"It's so hard to believe that he would do this. Gable worked so hard to get the hospital project up and running. And he's thrown it all away."

John nodded. He was still working through the issue of the hospital project. "It's a worthy cause, and many people in the community donated. Many of those people will want to see the project come to fruition, regardless of who heads it up. Something will be worked out in the end."

"So we still go to the charity ball, then?"

John smiled. "But of course. I want to see you in your new dress."

Jack couldn't help but chime in. "Me, too."

Isabelle found she could laugh. Then she sobered. "So how long do you think it will take to build a case against Gable?"

Jack answered. "I doubt I'll have all the evidence needed to have him arrested before the ball. And for the sake of the charity ball fundraiser, that might be for the best. The party will take place as scheduled. The money will come in, but once deposited, the first step will be to freeze the accounts. The cops will get the evidence I've compiled and add it to theirs. Gable will be arrested. He'll probably get out on bail, but he'll eventually see the inside of a prison."

Isabelle couldn't help but feel sorry for Gable's wife and daughter. "What about his family? They're going to be devastated."

Jack tried not to sound callous, but he'd been in this situation with other clients one too many times to feel the sympathy Isabelle did. "He did this to his family. And they will suffer because of it. Gable committed a white-collar crime, and it's his first offense. He'll play on the judge and jury's sympathies about his daughter who was burned in a fire and the debt that came of it. He'll most likely get off lightly if he plays his cards right and hires a really good lawyer."

John tried to soothe Isabelle. "Try not to think about it. Gable made his bed, and now he'll have to lie in it. And unfortunately, his wife and daughter are going to get caught in the backlash. There could be ways The Heart's Way could help minimize the impact on them, but we can't stop it."

Isabelle looked up into John's eyes. "I knew there was a reason I loved you. You stand up for the innocent."

John kissed her softly. "And I knew there was a reason I loved you. You have a compassionate heart."

Jack quietly left the room.

Chapter Twelve

The ball was in full swing, and so far, it was a resounding success. Pledges and donations had been pouring in since the presentation Gable had given. His wife and daughter had stood behind him, the scars his daughter bore visible for all to see. The trio made quite the picture of a family that had been struggling but overcoming life's circumstances.

Isabelle found it difficult to be around Gable. It was also difficult to stand around, smile, and make small talk when the fate of the project hung in the air. She had met with Stan, who had cheered her up some. She had met with other people in the city that she knew from her work at The Gables. She tried to be cheerful and optimistic in the presence of the donors. But every time her eye caught Gable talking to people, acting as if nothing was wrong, she wanted to confront him.

"You should stop glaring at him." John pressed his mouth near Isabelle's ear, the move meant to look like a kiss from a lover.

Isabelle nodded slightly. "It's so hard to believe he's guilty of embezzling. I worked for him for a year, and I never would have suspected. Every time I think about what he did, it just makes me so mad."

Since John could only agree, he kept silent. He scanned the room; most of the people were strangers to him. He saw some of his people, including Jack, who insisted on coming along, mingling in the crowd. Many of Gable's staff were not in attendance, as the fee for each guest charged by the hotel was significant.   Only key employees were in attendance from both foundations.

"Do you think anyone on the staff knows?" Isabelle turned away from Gable. She supposed the fact that he had accepted her resignation was reason enough to ignore him. Even if he had noticed her staring, she supposed Gable wouldn't suspect they knew what he had done.

"That's one of the reasons Jack wanted to come. He wants to see who Gable interacts with. So far, there haven't been any red flags. We ran preliminary background checks on everyone. Nothing suspicious."

"Except for me, apparently." Isabelle kissed his cheek to take the sting out of her words. It still irked her that he'd run such an extensive background search on her, but she understood why.

"You're a dangerous woman, Izzy." John cupped her chin in his palm.

She raised an eyebrow at that. "And how is that?"

John kissed her lightly. "The power a woman wields over a man can be a dangerous one. You've got my heart in the palm of your hand."

Isabelle melted against him. "So I have."

"Break it up, you two." Jack grinned at the pair. "You're supposed to be working."

Isabelle smiled at Jack but leaned closer into John. John

had a big grin on his face.

"We are working." John brought his arm around Isabelle's waist.

Jack took a sip of his champagne. How he wished he could have a beer instead. "So, I see. Well, people do enjoy a good love story. Two people, reunited after several years, find love amidst theft and intrigue. It makes for a good story. Once it breaks what Gable has done, The Heart's Way is going to have quite the task before it if you want to keep the hospital project underway. You two could be the new faces of the project."

John shrugged. "We have an excellent public relations team. They'll come up with something. The problem is with Gable gone, there won't be The Gables anymore. The Heart's Way was only assisting in the project, not spearheading it. And given the circumstances, I think it might be best if Isabelle and I pull ourselves out of the project."

Isabelle looked up in surprise. She knew John wasn't quite sure how the project would continue, but it had sounded like it would. "We're going to let the project die?"

"In its current state, yes. There are hundreds of people here tonight. Many of them are very influential. Trust me when I say that with the right approach and motivation, there is someone here tonight who will pick up the broken pieces of The Gables' legacy and get the project back underway. The Heart's Way will be more than happy to assist whoever that person may be. But I think it might be best if it weren't you and me. There are other project managers who are more than capable of seeing the project to fruition."

Isabelle considered that. The Heart's Way was full of people who could oversee the hospital project. And she knew John was right about someone stepping in. Some of the wealthiest people in the city were currently mingling in the ballroom. She knew many of them. "I suppose you have the right of it. And I wouldn't mind starting a new project as a full-time employee of The Heart's Way."

Jack looked at the pair, then directed his question to Isabelle. "You're staying in California, then?"

John nodded and spoke for her. "She's staying with me. I spoke with Emmett and he's ecstatic that Isabelle wants to join the foundation. And as soon as this fiasco is over, I'm planning on dedicating myself full-time to the project of convincing Isabelle to marry me."

Jack slapped John on the shoulder. "Good for you. It's about time you settled down and got married."

"Glad you approve, since you'll be the best man."

Jack's eyes widened for a moment, then they took on a mischievous gleam. "Never been a best man before. Can't wait to plan your bachelor party."

"I haven't said yes yet." Isabelle felt the need to remind John.

John stroked her cheek and enjoyed Isabelle's slight shiver. "You will."

"Until she does, we still have a job to do." Jack winked at Isabelle.

Jack had no doubt she'd say yes. The first time he'd seen the way John reacted to Isabelle, Jack knew John was down for the count. And honestly, Isabelle barely kept her eyes and hands off John. It was subtle, but the pair were always touching. Even now, John's arm was wrapped around Isabelle's waist, and Isabelle was leaning into him. Seeing them together reminded him of the brief time he'd been married and how happy he'd been so long ago.

Isabelle and John went back to mingling with the guests, answering questions about both foundations and how a project the size of a new hospital was going to take flight. Jack kept an eye on the crowd, seeing if anyone was giving any special attention to Gable or spending too much time avoiding him. So far, no one stood out. Jack was sure Gable was acting alone, but he'd been surprised before.

Isabelle left most of the talking to John. No one asked her straight out, but she had seen speculation in the eyes of the guests about how close she and John were. And since John was constantly holding her hand, touching her waist, or kissing her on the cheek or mouth, they were right in what they were thinking. But not one person commented, and she was grateful.

A couple of hours into the party, Isabelle excused herself. She headed toward the ladies' room. Halfway there, she thought she heard someone crying behind a closed door. She stopped and listened. Definitely crying. Unsure what to do, but not wanting to leave someone who might be sick or hurt, she knocked lightly on the door. The sound of crying stopped for a moment, but then picked back up.

Isabelle turned the knob, and the door opened easily. In the shadows of the room, she saw a small figure sitting on the floor, knees pulled to her chest. The pink sparkle of the dress was muted, but Isabelle had seen that dress earlier in the day. Brittany, Gable's daughter, was crying alone in an empty room.

Isabelle went into the room, closing the door behind her. Brittany was a regular fixture at the office. She came in from time to time, saying she wanted to help with whatever project was going on. Mostly the staff gave her some filing or some busy work, but Brittany, even at twelve, understood how important it was to give her time to help others.

Brittany looked up, tears streaming down her cheeks. "Daddy said you quit."

Isabelle took a seat next to her, heedless of her new, very expensive dress. "That's not why you're crying. Want to talk about it?"

"I probably shouldn't say. It's a secret."

Isabelle pulled a couple of tissues out of her purse. She handed them to the girl. "It must be some secret if it has you crying."

"It is. But it's a secret Mom wants me to keep from Dad. You have to promise not to tell."

"I promise." Isabelle brushed wet strands of hair from Brittany's face.

"Mom wants to leave. She wants to go someplace far away." Brittany wiped her eyes and nose.

"How come?" Isabelle thought about the implications of what this meant. Did Caitlyn know what her husband had done? Was she complicit, or wanting to get away from him and what he had done?

"She won't say why. She just says Daddy is going on a trip and won't be coming back. She says we can't stay here."

Brittany's tears fell harder.

Isabelle held Brittany as she cried. It took a few minutes before she calmed down. Isabelle took her to the bathroom and did what she could to reduce the girl's swollen eyes and tear-stained cheeks. Isabelle saw Brittany back safely to the ballroom and back under the wing of her mother.

Isabelle went to find John and Jack. When she spotted John, she calmly walked up to him and tucked her arm in his while he spoke to a donor. She glanced around the room and saw Jack chatting with a tall redhead. She wasn't sure how to get his attention, but he must have realized she wanted to talk to him because she saw him excuse himself and head her way.

John didn't bother to ask if something was wrong when Jack came over. He excused himself from the person he had been chatting with. "I think we've been here long enough. Our duty is done."

"Agreed." Jack led the two of them out of the ballroom.

John said goodbye to people in passing. He caught Gable's eye and simply nodded. When the man waved back, John escorted Isabelle to the elevators. Since they were staying in the hotel where the party was being held, the trio quickly made their way upstairs. With an unspoken agreement, they met in Jack's room. He had his computer ready and waiting.

Jack kicked off his shoes and loosened his tie. "So what happened?"

John led Isabelle to the nearest bed and sat her down. "Something obviously upset you. And you were gone for quite a while. Did someone approach you?"

Isabelle shook her head. "Nothing like that. I was headed for the ladies' room, and I heard someone crying. Brittany was hiding out in a room near the bathrooms."

"Brittany, as in Gable's daughter?" Jack had seen the young girl earlier in the evening. She had been wearing a knee-length pink dress. Jack thought it extremely distasteful that a father would show his daughter's disfigured legs for his own gain. The girl had been uncomfortable on stage earlier that evening.

"Yes. And she said the oddest thing. She said she had to keep a secret from her father. She said her mother was making them go away. And then she said that her daddy was going on a trip and wouldn't be back."

John turned to Jack. "It's possible Caitlyn, Gable's wife, is aware of what Gable is doing. Maybe you should try to corner her."

Jack flipped open the lid on this laptop. "It's possible she does. It can be hard to hide money troubles from a spouse. Especially if the spouse is used to spending money at will. Caitlyn Lockwood was wearing some very expensive jewelry this evening. And though I'm no expert, I'd guess her dress cost a pretty penny as well."

Isabelle nodded. "No doubt. I like Caitlyn, but she is not shy about her spending habits. The house they share is massive, and it's filled to the rafters with expensive things, both hers and Gable's. Gable started up his foundation using his own cash. After his daughter was injured, he quit working for some time, and it was during that time that he came up with the idea of The Gables. Caitlyn doesn't spend much time at the office but is active when it comes to fundraising."

"If we do confront her, you should be there Isabelle. She'll be more comfortable with a woman present." Jack punched a few keys on his computer, not taking his attention away from what he was doing.

Isabelle looked from Jack to John. Both men were tall, though Jack was much more so. But both men would easily intimidate a woman like Caitlyn, who, from what Isabelle could tell, lived a sheltered life.

"I suppose confronting Caitlyn will be the quickest way to get answers." Isabelle kicked off her heels and began massaging her aching feet.

John pulled Isabelle's legs onto his lap and took over the task. "I'll reschedule our flight, and the two of us can go to the house tomorrow. I spoke with Gable this evening, and he's expected to attend a brunch, so he won't be home. When I asked him if the whole family was attending, he said they would still be asleep when he left the house."

Isabelle bit back a moan. "You were planning on confronting her already, weren't you?"

"Yes. Jack is digging, but sometimes you have to talk to people face to face. I didn't want to tip off Gable, but given the fact that he has to know Marcus was arrested, he has to know Marcus is likely to tell the whole tale to the police."

Jack looked up from his computer. "The police are in the process of freezing his accounts as we speak. Brittany said her daddy was going on a trip. Gable is planning to cut his losses and flee."

Isabelle still had a hard time believing Gable had stolen

money. And she couldn't believe he would up and leave his family. "But what about his wife and daughter? He's spent the last few years building the foundation, and his daughter is the reason."

Jack had no sympathy. "He's looking out for number one now, and that's himself. And I'm guessing when you talk to Caitlyn tomorrow, you'll find the picture-perfect family we saw tonight is a ruse."

John set Isabelle's legs aside and pulled her to her feet. "Either way, this will come to a head. We just have to gather what evidence we can, and the police will do the rest."

Isabelle let John lead her back to their room, her heart heavy.

* * *

"I knew something was wrong, but I didn't know what. I thought he was cheating, so I hired a private investigator." Caitlyn Lockwood dabbed her eyes with a tissue, her eyes pleading with John and Isabelle, who sat on the couch across from her.

"And he didn't find a lover, but something else." John handed Caitlyn a fresh tissue. He was having a difficult time masking his impatience.

"He found large cash deposits in our accounts. He also found that all of our credit cards were maxed out and that Gable had taken out a personal loan. I gave the investigator access to the foundation's accounts. That's when he told me Gable had been stealing from the foundation. I didn't know what to do. Then he found out Gable had booked a flight to

Mexico for the end of the month. He's planning to leave me."

Isabelle couldn't temper the anger in her voice. "But why would you tell your daughter? Your daughter was crying alone at the ball last night, terribly distraught about her father leaving and you two moving away."

Caitlyn looked up from the mangled tissue. "She might as well learn early in life that you can't trust anyone, not even her father. He was going to up and leave us without a word. We have to go; the scandal of it all will ruin me. Gable will get on a plane in two days, and we'll get on one too."

John rose. "Don't bet on it."

Isabelle trailed behind John as they quickly left the house. "Do you think she'll tell him we were here?"

"Not likely. However, I wouldn't put it past her to pack up her and her daughter and catch the next flight out to whatever destination it is she has in mind." John held open the car door for Isabelle.

"It's so hard to believe she'll just pack and go."

"She might not be able to, unless she has an account without Gable's name on it. While we were talking to her, Jack texted that all the accounts are now frozen. But if she was able to hire an investigator without her husband's knowledge, then I'm guessing she has some cash stashed. And Gable won't get out of the country. The airport has been alerted not to let Gable on the plane if the police don't get to him today."

When John's phone beeped, Isabelle picked it up while John drove them back to the hotel.

"Well?" John pulled onto the freeway.

"It's Jack. Marcus cut a deal and spilled his guts to the police. He told them Gable paid him to vandalize the warehouse. He even admitted to attacking you and vandalizing my apartment. Must have been some deal."

"Most likely. He was looking at jail time for parole violation at a minimum. Probably figured if he played his cards right, he'd get his sentence reduced. What else does Jack say?"

Isabelle swiped the screen. "Just that the police now have a warrant for Gable's arrest and are looking for him. The police have all the evidence Jack collected, and with Marcus's deal sealed, the police now have a solid case against Gable."

John watched as Isabelle put his phone away. She had an odd look on her face. "What are you thinking?"

Isabelle looked up at John. "Brittany. My father was not a nice man. Neither was his father. Marcus followed in their footsteps. On the surface, Gable was the perfect father. But he turned out to be an embezzler and was planning to leave his wife and daughter behind. Brittany has had a hard life. I can't help but wonder if one day she'll end up following in her father's footsteps the way Marcus did."

John spoke softly, his eyes on the road. "Or maybe she'll go the opposite. Do what you did, and refuse to become a victim, or use the excuse of having a lousy childhood to do whatever you want. No one made your brother become a criminal. He made that choice. You had the same parents, and here you are working for an organization founded on the idea of helping others. Brittany has the same choice ahead of her that we all do. In the end, she'll be fine. Gable might have gone astray, but his heart started in the right place."

Isabelle relaxed and closed her eyes. "Brittany has a good heart. One can only hope her mother will nurture it in the hard days ahead. What is our next move?"

"My next move is to take you back to the hotel and let you take a nap. You've hardly slept the past week. Jack and I are going to join the hunt to find Gable."

Isabelle thought about protesting, but crawling into the overstuffed bed at the hotel sounded a lot more appealing than watching Jack play around on his computer while John paced the room. Though both men were nice to look at, she was exhausted. It had been hard to sleep. Her brother was going back to jail, someone she had considered a friend was going to end up there, and she was fighting herself when it came to her relationship with John. He had brought up marriage again last night as they lay in bed. As usual, sex had relaxed both of them, and John used the opportunity to ask her again. She had a feeling she was going to keep hearing the question until she gave him the answer he wanted.

They arrived back at the hotel, and John led Isabelle to the elevators. "I'm meeting Jack in the lounge. Text me if you need me. And get some rest."

Isabelle turned her face up for a kiss. She couldn't help but cup his cheek and let the kiss linger. When she pulled away, John's eyes were heated, but he took a step back and just watched as the elevator doors slid closed.

Isabelle leaned against the back of the elevator, her belly in knots. She just wanted this to be over. The doors slid open, and she headed for the room she and John were sharing. Sighing, she slipped the card into the lock and let the door gently close behind her.

Chapter Thirteen

"So where do you think he's hiding?" John wasn't half as good on a computer as Jack, but he was determined to find Gable so he and Isabelle could go home.

"He's not at the warehouse, and he's not at the office. And we know he's not at home. The police are watching all three locations. Surveillance at the hotel shows him leaving and not returning, so he's not here." Jack took a sip of the drink the very lovely, and the very interested, waitress had left him.

"As far as I can tell, he doesn't have very many friends or places that are not work-related that he would go. He could have paid cash and is staying near the airport." John continued going through Gable's accounts for any recent activity or attempts to withdraw money, but so far there had been none.

Jack nodded. "Guys more of a recluse than I am, and I haven't been out much lately. Gable Lockwood is even more obsessed with his job than I am."

"You could be right. I haven't known him long, but outside of work, he never made any attempts at making friends."

Jack nodded again, his eyes still glued to his screen. "You don't have money to give him. As far as I can tell, the only people he socializes with donates big money to the foundation."

John growled in frustration. "Yet no one has seen him, no one has heard from him, and Gable has to know by now the cops are looking for him. He wouldn't have disappeared otherwise."

"And his wife didn't seem to have any information to add. By the way, she has a flight booked for her and her daughter that leaves in a few hours. I had someone at the office see where she was going, and it looks like they're headed to her mother's house across the country."

John figured she wasn't going to stick around any longer than necessary. "She wants to be long gone when this hits the press. Gable will make the news tonight, assuming he's found."

"We'll find him." Jack's brows furrowed.

"What?" John noticed Jack's sudden interest in his computer.

"He's here."

"Where here?"

Jack closed the lid quickly and rose. "I've been tracking Gable's phone. It just turned on. He's somewhere here in the hotel."

John rose and ran for the elevators. Isabelle was alone twelve stories up.

Jack had just enough time to squeeze through the elevator doors before they closed behind him.

* * *

As soon as the door had closed behind her, she headed to the bath. She splashed some cool water on her cheeks to help clear her head. When she looked in the mirror, the dark circles under her eyes were more pronounced than they had been the day before. It was no wonder John wanted her to rest.

After leaving the bath, Isabelle headed for the curtains, intending to pull them closed to block out the light. She already had the do not disturb sign on the door, so she hoped for some peace and quiet for the rest of the afternoon. She knew John and Jack wouldn't rest until they found Gable.

"That will certainly make this easier." Gable stepped out from the corner of the room where he had hidden. Given the layout of the room, Isabelle hadn't been able to see him from the entryway.

Isabelle heard Gable's voice, and her hand stilled on the curtains. It hadn't occurred to her that he might come looking for her.

"Go ahead and pull them closed. This won't take long, but we don't need an audience."

"Why are you here?" Isabelle turned to see Gable standing in the corner, a very large knife in his hand. Trembling, she pulled the curtains closed. Gable had turned the lights on, so she could still see him.

"You're going to be my way out. Believe me when I say this wasn't how I wanted it to be." Gable crossed the space to stand between Isabelle and the door. The knife was held to his side.

Isabelle felt the trembling move from her hands to her

legs but knew she needed to stay calm and not panic. "I don't see how I can help you."

"You're the reason Marcus is in jail, or I should say your boyfriend is the reason. I would have gone to Marcus for this final job, but since I can't, you're going to have to be the one."

"Killing me won't accomplish anything." Isabelle stayed as far from him as she could, her back to the wall.

"I suppose if I killed you, John would be bound and determined to return the favor. But I have a feeling his friend Jack, or the cops, would keep him from doing that. They'd rather I spend my days locked up. But I have no intention of going to jail. And don't worry, I don't plan to kill you. You're going to kill me."

Isabelle could hardly understand what he was saying to her. "I won't kill you."

Gable held up the knife. "But you will, my dear, or I will kill you. Look over at the table beside you."

Not wanting to take her eyes off Gable, but knowing she needed to look, Isabelle forced herself to glance at the table. A large, black gun lay on it. She shook her head in denial.

"I know it's been done before in movies, so I can't take the credit. But if the cops find me, I will go to prison. My passport and all my assets are frozen, so unless I steal a car and rob a bank, I'm not getting out of the country. I can't kill myself, or my wife and daughter won't get my insurance money. I can't risk the insurance claim being nullified if the cops shoot me, so you're going to have to do it. But don't worry, it will be self-defense. You won't go to jail."

"You think I'm just going to shoot you?" Isabelle held up a hand when he took a step closer, the knife held out.

"Yes, I do. It really will be self-defense. If you don't shoot me, I will use this knife on you. I've got nothing else to lose. Pick up the gun, Isabelle."

Isabelle shook her head. "I won't do this."

Gable crossed to her and picked up the gun. He shoved it into her hands. He then pulled out his cell phone. He punched a few buttons. "Caitlyn, when you hear this, I'll be gone. I need you to know how much I love you and Brittany. I know you won't believe me, but I stole that money for us, to make our lives better. I thought when I took it, I'd be able to repay it. But things didn't quite work out the way they were supposed to."

Isabelle watched as Gable took a deep breath and spoke into the phone again.

"Brittany, I need you to know that Daddy loves you, and none of this is your fault. I wanted so badly to make you better, and I was willing to spend whatever it took to see that your body and mind were healed. I should have paid more attention to you; I should have listened to you more. You're beautiful just the way you are. Be sure to mind your mother and know that we both only want what's best for you."

Gable tossed the phone on the bed. "Make sure they get that."

Isabelle glanced at the phone, then at the gun in her hand. "Gable, this isn't the way. Your wife and daughter need you. Yes, you'll go to jail, but it won't be forever. You can make amends; you can still be there for them. Believe me, I know."

"What do you know?" Gable lifted the knife and took a step toward Isabelle.

"My father overdosed rather than face what he had done. He had destroyed the business his father had built, and he had taken to using drugs. But he could have gotten help; he could still be with us today. He could have made amends and turned his life around. But he chose the easy way out. What you need to do is own up to what you've done, pay the price, and then get on with your life, doing whatever you have to do to make this up to your wife and daughter."

"Caitlyn wants a divorce. She filed over a month ago. There is nothing left to go back to. And Brittany will be better off with a big insurance payoff than she will be living with her father in prison."

Isabelle shook her head. "You're wrong. And I won't shoot you."

"But you will." Gable lifted the knife, using it to make a deep wound on Isabelle's arm that held the gun.

Isabelle gasped and closed her fingers over the blood that was pouring out of her arm. "Don't do this."

"I have to. Raise the gun, Isabelle."

Isabelle managed to sidestep when Gable made a swing at her with his knife. This time, with her hands trembling, she raised the gun. "Please don't do this."

"Do it for Brittany." Gable took another swing, this time slicing through the sleeve of her blouse on her bicep.

Isabelle clamped her fingers over the fresh wound. She saw Gable raise the knife as if to stab her in the chest.

Knowing he had no intention of stopping and realizing Gable meant to kill her if she didn't obey, Isabelle raised the gun. She felt tears streaming down her cheeks, but it wasn't from the cuts on her arm. She put her finger on the trigger, prepared to squeeze as Gable came at her one last time.

"Stop!" John burst through the door, quickly realizing what was happening. He tackled Gable.

Jack had a gun, and he trained it on Gable as John pinned the man to the floor. But the battle was quickly over as Gable began to cry.

John glanced over at Jack, and Jack pulled out zip-tie restraints and handed them to John. John quickly tied his arms, and he and Jack yanked Gable to his feet.

Jack pulled Gable from the room, taking him down the hall. The police were on their way, but Jack wanted to get Gable away from Isabelle.

John was breathing heavily from the scuffle. "Are you okay?"

Isabelle dropped the gun on the floor and ran over to John. She threw herself into his arms but let out a cry when she lifted her arm.

"What's wrong?" John set her back and saw the blood pouring down her arm.

"He cut me." Isabelle heard the words, but they came from a distance. She had a feeling she was about to faint.

John caught her as she collapsed in his arms.

* * *

Isabelle woke as voices called to her. The loudest and

most annoying voice was John's. She opened her eyes but quickly closed them when a bright light shone in them.

"Come on, Izzy, open your eyes." John squeezed her hand, willing her to obey.

She opened her eyes again, focusing on John. She realized there were a couple of paramedics hovering over her, and one of them was shining a light in her eyes.

"Welcome back." The young man switched the light off as another man bandaged her arm.

She kept her eyes on Jack as the two men asked her questions about how she felt and her medical history. She answered them, but tears kept threatening, and her throat kept closing up.

"You'll be fine. You've had a shock, and you need rest."

"I don't want to go to the hospital." Isabelle looked at John, her eyes pleading.

"Sorry, Izzy. I want you to go. They're going to clean the wound better and get you some medicine so you don't get an infection. I promise I'll get you out of there as soon as the doctor says you can go."

Isabelle nodded and let the men get her onto the gurney. She saw Jack in the hallway, and he came over as they passed by.

Jack leaned over and kissed her cheek. "We've got Gable in custody, and I'll be right behind you."

Isabelle nodded and closed her eyes. She was feeling a little lightheaded, so she was pretty sure the paramedic had given her something for the pain. The cuts were a dull ache right now, but she had a feeling they were going to hurt a lot worse later.

Nurses, doctors, and then police officers came and went over the next couple of hours. She answered all of their questions. Both John and Jack were with her while she relayed her story to the police. She knew Gable was in custody. She wasn't sure what new charges would be brought, but she had no doubt new charges would be leveled against him. She supposed assault with a deadly weapon would be one of them, or perhaps attempted murder.

It was a couple of hours later, after the police left and the doctor cleared her to go home, that she was finally allowed to leave. John made arrangements at a different hotel. Jack left to fetch their things. John had decided to delay their flight for a couple of days so she could rest up before the flight home. Jack had made arrangements for the next flight out so he could get back to work.

Isabelle couldn't help but enjoy it as John fussed over her. Jack had delivered their luggage, then went to his room next door. John had helped her into her nightgown and helped her settle under the covers.

"How did Gable get into our room?" It was one of the questions that bothered her.

"He had been in and out of that hotel so much with the parties that he held there; he had gotten his hands on a master key. Apparently, he'd had it since the night of the party. I'm not sure what he intended to do with it when he stole it, but that's how he got in. The hotel didn't realize it was missing."

"I suppose Caitlyn and Brittany are already on a flight out of town."

"They were detained by the police for questioning, but they'll be out on the next one available. The police have cleared Caitlyn of any wrongdoing, and Gable confessed to everything. I've no doubt he's hoping if he's cooperative, the judge will go easy on him."

Isabelle heard the anger in John's voice and grabbed his hand to hold it to her chest. "I'm just glad it's all over now. I just want to go home."

"As soon as you're feeling better, I'll book us a flight. But you need to rest." John shifted her over until he could climb into bed beside her. It wasn't an easy feat since she refused to release his hand.

Isabelle pressed up against him, tucking his hand between her breasts. "So now what do we do?"

John kissed her, then pulled her into his arms. "If you agree to marry me, we can live happily ever after."

Isabelle smiled against his chest. "I love you."

John kissed the top of her head. "I love you. So, will you?"

"Yes, John. I'll marry you."

John released her and left the bed.

Confused, Isabelle tried to sit up, but it was too much of a strain on her arm. "Most men would have stayed in bed and made love to me."

John grinned. He went to his suitcase. "I've been waiting for you to say yes since I asked you the first time."

"Which was only a little less than two weeks ago." She lay back and enjoyed the view of her naked fiancé as he dug through his bag.

"I paid extra to have it resized quickly, so I'd have it

when you said yes. I hope you like traditional."

Isabelle looked away from his body to the hand he held out to her. In it lay a traditional engagement ring. It was a solitaire, square-cut diamond, and she loved it. She held out her left hand so he could slip it on.

"It's beautiful. I can't believe you've had this in your bag."

John climbed back into bed. "I've had this on me since two days after I asked you the first time. We'll pick wedding bands out together when we get back."

Isabelle admired the ring for a moment. It was quite stunning. And so was the man who had given it to her.

"Are you going to make love to me now?" Isabelle rolled onto her back, holding out her good arm.

"Definitely." John eased his body over hers, careful not to move her arm.

"I do love you, John. I loved you as a child loves, and I love you now as a woman loves."

"And I love you, Izzy. For now and always."

<u>From The Author</u>

I hope you enjoyed the first book in my series, The Heart's Way. All books in the series can be read alone, but I always think it's more fun to read them in order. Get the next title in the four-book series, Ask Me To, for Jack's story, as well as books three and four, Say You Love Me and Forever Love, at your favorite retailer.

If you enjoyed the book and would like an email on my next release, please sign up for my newsletter @ elizabeth-castle.com/contact. Please be assured that your email will never be sold (I wouldn't want mine sold, so I wouldn't do that to someone else). You can also follow me on Facebook @ facebook.com/elizabethcastle.romanceauthor

Also, if you enjoyed this book, or any of my other titles, please consider leaving a rating at your favorite retailer, Goodreads and/or Bookbub. And if you have the time, a text review would be lovely. Indie authors rely on readers like you to tell others how much you enjoy their books.

Happy reading,

Elizabeth Castle

Books by Elizabeth Castle

Single Titles:
    Going Home
    This Kind Of Love
    Chasing Hope
    The Babe & The Librarian (novella)

The Heart's Way Series:
    For Now and Always
    Ask Me To
    Say You Love Me
    Forever Love

Bennett Family Series:
    This Time Love
    A Bride For David (novella)

All Of Me Series:
    All Of My Days
    All Of My Nights

Cantwell Quartet Series:
    Falling Slowly
    Unraveled
    Hidden Away
    Entangled

Contemporary "Retro" Romance Series:
    Loving Jordan

Visit elizabeth-castle.com for newsletter sign up and up-to-date releases.